INTO THE UNDERGROUND

"It's not too far," she said, walking quickly along the dark street. Nothing else was said until she reached a grimy apartment building not far from the Thames. Sara unlocked the door, waved him through, then led the way to her rooms.

"It's good to see you you again, Jan Kulozik."

"And you, Sara. A little different from the first time."

"We do seem to meet under unusual circumstances—but these are unusual times . . ."

"Welcome to London. What do you want from me?"

Before Sara could answer, there was a rapid beeping from the turned-off radio. She was on her feet in an instant, running swiftly into the other room. "Take your jacket off, open your shirt," she called back over her shoulder. She returned in a few moments wearing a very transparent black gown trimmed with pink lace. There was a knock at the door.

"Who is it?" she asked, calling through the thin paneling.

"Police," was the short, shocking answer . . .

Bantam Books by Harry Harrison
Ask your bookseller for the books you have missed

HOMEWORLD
THE STAINLESS STEEL RAT WANTS YOU!
STARWORLD
WHEELWORLD

HOMEWORLD

Harry Harrison

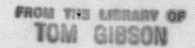

HOMEWORLD
A Bantam Book / November 1980
2nd printing .... November 1980
3rd printing .... July 1981

ISBN 0-553-20247-2

Published simultaneously in the United States and Canada

Bantam Books are published by Bantam Books, Inc. Its trademark, consisting of the words "Bantam Books" and the por-
trayal of a rooster, is Registered in U.S. Patent and Trademark
Office and in other countries. Marca Registrada. Bantam
Books, Inc., 666 Fifth Avenue, New York, New York 10103.

PRINTED IN THE UNITED STATES OF AMERICA

12 11 10 9 8 7 6 5 4 3

HOMEWORLD

One

"It's a monstrosity, a bastard combination of antique piping, worn valves—and modern electronic technology. The whole thing should be blown up and built over from scratch."

"Not that bad, your honor, I think, not really that bad." Radcliffe rubbed his reddened nose with the back of his hand, looked up guiltily when he saw it streaked and wet. The tall engineer beside him had not noticed; Radcliffe wiped it surreptitiously on his trouser leg. "It works, we produce a fine spirit . . ."

"It works—but just barely." Jan Kulozik was tired and there was a sharp edge to his voice. "All of the packing glands should be replaced at once or it will blow itself up without any help from me. Look at those leaks, puddles of the stuff."

"I'll have it cleaned up at once, your honor."

"That's not what I mean. Stop the leaks in the first place. Do something constructive, man. That's an order."

"As you say, so shall it be done."

Radcliffe lowered his head obediently, trembling. Jan looked down on the man's balding head, the dusting of dandruff on the fringe of oily hair, and could feel only disgust. These people never learned. They could not think for themselves and even when ordered

1

to do the correct thing made a mess of it half of the time. This manager was about as efficient as the collection of ancient fractioning columns, fermenting vats, and rusty pipes that made up this vegetable-fuel plant. It seemed a waste of time to install the automation controls.

Cold winter light from the tall windows barely outlined the dark mechanical shapes inside the building; spotlights made pools of yellow across the floor. One of the workmen shuffled into view, paused, and groped through his pockets. The motion caught Jan's eye.

"That man—stop!" he shouted.

The command was sudden, startling. The workman had not known the engineer was there. He dropped the match—even before he had lit the joint— and it fell into the pool of liquid at his feet. Sudden blue flame leaped high.

Jan shouldered the man aside roughly as he jumped for the fire extinguisher, tearing it from the bracket, pounding the release as he ran. The workman was stamping wildly at the pool of burning alcohol which only served to spread the flame.

Foam coughed out of the extinguisher's mouth and Jan directed it down, around. The fire was out in a moment, but the workman's trousers were smoldering. Jan whipped the foam across the man's legs and then, in a fit of anger, up his legs, chest, splashing and coating his face with a white blanket.

"You're an absolute fool, a total fool!"

Jan turned off the valve and threw the extinguisher down. The workman was gasping and wiping his eyes; Jan looked on coldly.

"You know smoking is forbidden in here. You must have been told often enough. And you're standing right under a *no smoking* sign."

2

"I . . . I don't read so well, your honor." He choked and spat out the bitter liquid.

"Not so well, or probably not at all. You're fired, get out of here."

"No, please, your honor, don't say that," the man wailed, the pain in his eyes forgotten, his mouth a gaping O of despair. "I've worked hard—my family—the dole for years . . ."

"The dole for life," Jan said coldly, the anger drained away as he looked at the man before him, on his knees in the foam. "Just be happy that I'm not preferring sabotage charges."

The situation was almost impossible. Jan stamped away, unaware of the staring eyes of the manager and the silent workmen. Just impossible. But better in the control room. Much better. He could almost relax, smile, as he looked at the shining order of the system he had installed. Cable conduits snaked in from all sides, merging and joining together at the control unit. He pressed the keys on the combination lock in sequence and the cover swung open. Silent, smooth, and perfect. The microcomputer in the heart of the machine ran everything with infinite precision. The terminal hung in its holster from his belt. He unclipped it and plugged it into the computer, tapped out a message on the keys. The screen lit up in instant response. No problems, not here. Though of course that wasn't the case elsewhere in the plant. When he asked for a general condition report the lines of readout went marching by.

VALVE UNIT 376–L–9 LEAKING
VALVE UNIT 389–P–6 IN NEED OF REPLACEMENT
VALVE UNIT 429–P–8 LEAKING

It was all thoroughly depressing and he cleared the screen with a quick command. Behind him Radcliffe's voice spoke quietly, respectfully from the open door.

"Please excuse me, Engineer Kulozik, but it is about Simmons, the man you fired. He's a good worker."

"I don't think he's very good." The anger was drained now and Jan wanted to be reasonable about this. But firm. "There will be plenty of people queuing up for his job. Any one of them will do it as well—or better."

"He studied for years, your honor. Years. To get off the dole. That shows something."

"Lighting that match showed even more. I'm sorry. I'm not a cruel man. But I'm thinking of you and the others here. What would you do if he burned down *your* jobs. You're management, Radcliffe, and that's the way you must think. It may be hard, and look wrong from the outside, but it is the only thing to do. You agree, don't you?"

There was a slight hesitation, but the answer came.

"Of course. You're right. I'm sorry I bothered you. I'll get him out of here now. We can't have his kind around."

"That's the way to do it."

A soft buzz and a flashing red light from the control unit drew Jan's attention; Radcliffe hesitated in the doorway. The computer had found something wrong and wanted Jan to know about it, displaying the information.

VALVE UNIT 928–R–9 IS NOW INOPERATIVE IN PERMANENTLY OPEN CONDITION. IT HAS BEEN ISOLATED FOR REPLACEMENT.

"928-R. Sounds familiar." Jan tapped the information into his personal computer and nodded. "I thought so. That thing was supposed to have been replaced last week. Was the job completed?"

"I'll have to check the records." Radcliffe was pale.

"Don't bother. We both know it wasn't done. So get out of here and get a valve and we will do the job *now*."

Jan himself detached the motor drive unit, using a power wrench on the recalcitrant lugnuts. They were heavy with rust. Typical. It had apparently been too much effort to put some oil on them before they had been tightened. He stood aside and watched closely while the sweating proles struggled to get the old valve off, splashing through the runnels of liquid that ran from the pipe end. When the new unit had been fitted and tightened into place under his attentive eye—no second-rate job this time—he bolted on the motor drive. The work was done efficiently without any extra chatter and the workmen picked up their tools and left as soon as it was finished. Jan went back to control to open the blocked section and get the plant functioning again. Once more he had the condition report scroll by, then had a hard copy made. When it had emerged from the printer he dropped into a chair to go through it carefully, ticking off the items that seemed to need the most urgent attention. He was a tall, almost gangling man, in his late twenties. Women thought him good looking—a number had told him so—but he did not think it particularly important. They were nice but they had their place. Which was immediately after microcircuit engineering. Whenever he read he frowned so that an almost permanent crease was stamped between his eyes. He frowned even more now as he went through the list a second time—then burst into a wide grin.

"Done—just about done!"

What should have been a simple job here at the

Walsoken Plant had stretched on and on. It had been autumn when he had arrived to make the control installation, along with Buchanan, an hydraulics engineer. But Buchanan had had the bad luck—good luck really—to be laid low by an attack of appendicitis and had been spirited away by ambulance copter never to return. Nor had his replacement ever arrived. Jan had found himself supervising the mechanical installation in addition to his own electronics and autumn had stretched into winter with no end in sight.

It was in sight now. All of the major installations and repairs had been done; the plant was up and running. And he was going to get out. For a few weeks at least—and the manager would just have to fend for himself.

"Radcliffe, get in here. I have some interesting news for you."

The words cracked from every loudspeaker in the building, rolled and echoed. Within seconds there was the sound of running footsteps and the panting manager came hurrying into the room.

"Yes . . . your honor?"

"I'm leaving. Today. Don't gape, man, I thought you would be pleased at the prospect. This antique vodka works is on line and should keep on running if you take care of all the maintenance on this list. I've hooked the computer through the network to fuelconcent where the operation will be monitored. Any problems will bring someone here fast. But I don't expect any problems, do I, Radcliffe?"

"No, sir, of course not. Do our best, thank you, sir."

"I hope so. And may your best be a little bit better than it has been in the past. I'll be back as soon as I am able, to check operation and to see your list of completion. Now—unless there is anything else—I am going to get out of this place."

"No. Nothing, sir."

"Good. See that it stays that way."

Jan waved the manager out as he unclipped his terminal and computer and stowed them in his case. Eagerly, for the first time it seemed, he pulled on the fleece-lined coat and driving gloves. One stop at the hotel to pack his bag and that was that! He whistled between his teeth as he slammed out of the door into the late afternoon gloom. The ground was frozen hard as rock and there was the smell of snow in the air. His car, red and shining, was the only touch of color in the drab landscape. Blighted fields stretched away on all sides in the flat landscape, silent under the drab gray sky. The fuel cell fired as soon as he turned the key; the heater warmed the interior with a rush of air. He drove slowly over the frozen ruts of the yard and out onto the paved road.

This was former fen country, now drained and plowed. But some of the old canals were still there; Wisbech was still an inland port. He would be glad to see the last of it. Packing took ten minutes—he believed in traveling light—and the manager held the front door and bowed him out and wished him a safe journey.

Just outside of town the motorway began. The police at the entrance saluted and he returned them an airy wave. Once on the automated road network he switched over to automatic, giving LONDON EXIT 74 as his destination. This information flashed from the transmitter under his car to the cable buried beneath the surface, to the network computer which routed him and sent back the command to the car computer in microseconds. There was a slow surge of acceleration by the electric wheel motors up to the standard 240 K.P.H., until the landscape became a blur in the gathering dusk. Jan had no desire to look out at it. He unlocked his seat and swiveled it about to face the

7

rear. There was whiskey ready in the bar compartment and water at the touch of a button. The television came on to a colorful and loud production of Peter Grimes. Jan enjoyed it for a minute, admiring the soprano not only for her voice—and tried to think whom she reminded him of.

"Aileen Pettit—of course!" He had a warm glow of memory; if she were only free now. She had little enough to do since her divorce. She should jump at the chance to see him. To think was to act. He punched for phone, then tapped her number quickly into the keys. It rang only twice before she answered.

"Jan. How nice of you to call."

"How nice of you to answer. Do you have camera trouble?" He pointed at his own dark screen.

"No, just blanked for privacy. You caught me in the sauna."

The screen came to life as she said this and she laughed at his expression. "Never saw a nude woman before?"

"If I have I've forgotten. They don't have women where I've been. At least none glowing and wet like you. Honestly, Aileen, I could almost weep for joy. You're the most beautiful sight in the world."

"Flattery will get you everywhere."

"And you're coming with me. Are you free now?"

"Always free, my love, but it depends on what you have in mind."

"Some sunshine. Some hot sun and warm ocean and good food, a case of champagne and you. What do you say?"

"I say it sounds unspeakably lovely. My bank account or yours?"

"My treat. I deserve something after this winter in the wilderness. I know this little hotel, right out in the desert on the shore of the Red Sea. If we leave in the morning we can get there . . ."

"No details, please, my sweet. I'm going to sink back into my sauna and wait there for you. Don't be too long."

She broke the connection with the last word and Jan laughed out loud. Yes, life was going to be a lot better. He drained the glass of scotch and poured another one.

The frozen fen country was already gone from his mind.

He did not know that the man he had fired, Simmons, never would go back on the dole. He committed suicide just about the time Jan reached London.

Two

The circular shadow of the great flying ship drifted slowly over the blue surface of the Mediterranean far below, across the beach and onto the desert beyond. The electric motors were silent, the only sound the whir of the propellers. They were tiny, almost lost from sight under the thick, saucerlike form of the *Beachy Head*, for their only work was to propel her through the air. Lift was supplied by the helium bags concealed beneath the taut outer skin. The dirigible was a superior form of transportation with very low fuel consumption.

Her cargo consisted of great bundles of heavy black pipes slung beneath the body. Tons of them. But the *Beachy Head* carried passengers as well, in cabins in the bow.

"The view is incredible," Aileen said, sitting before the angled window that made up the entire front wall of their cabin, watching the desert move by below. Jan, stretched out on the bed, nodded in silent agreement—but was looking at her. She was combing her shoulder-length coppery-red hair, her raised arms lifting her bare breasts, her back arched and lovely.

"Incredible," he said, and she laughed and put down the comb to come and sit beside him and kiss him.

10

"Marry me?" Jan asked.

"Thank you, no. My divorce isn't a month old. I want to enjoy my freedom for a while yet."

"I'll ask you next month."

"Do that . . ." The chiming bell cut her off and the steward's voice broke the silence of the cabin.

"All passengers. We will be landing in Suez in thirty minutes' time. Please have your bags ready for the porters. Thirty minutes' time. It has been our pleasure to have you aboard the *Beachy Head* and in the name of Captain Wetherby and the crew I want to thank you for flying British Airways."

"A half an hour and look at my hair! And I haven't started packing yet . . ."

"There's no hurry. And no one will throw you out of the cabin. This is a holiday, remember? I'm going to get dressed and see about the luggage. I'll meet you on the ground."

"Can't you wait for me?"

"I'll be waiting—but outside. I want to see what kind of drilling gear they are unloading."

"You care more about all those filthy pipes than you do about me."

"Absolutely correct——how did you find out? But this is a momentous occasion. If the thermal extraction techniques work, we may be pumping oil again. For the first time in over two-hundred years."

"Oil? From where?" Aileen's voice was distant; she was more interested in getting the thin blouse over her head.

"The ground. It used to be there, a lot of it, petroleum. Pumped dry by the Wreckers, oxidized and wasted just like everything else. A really beautiful source of chemical hydrocarbons that they just burned up."

"I haven't the slightest idea of what you are talking about. I always failed history."

11

"See you on the ground."

When Jan stepped out of the lift at the foot of the mooring tower, he felt as though he had walked through the open door of an oven. Even in the middle of winter the sun had a bite unknown in the north. After his exile in the frozen fens it felt good.

Bundles of pipes were being lowered now by the cable hoists. Drifting down slowly, bobbing slightly under the buoyant airship, dropping again to clang onto the waiting flatbed truck. For a moment Jan thought of applying for permission to visit the well site—then changed his mind. No. Holiday first. Perhaps on the way back. For the time being he must cleanse his mind of the glories of science and technology, and instead explore the more fascinating glories of Aileen Pettit.

When she appeared from the lift they strolled to the customs building hand in hand, enjoying the feel of the sun on their skin. A solemn, dark-skinned policeman stood guard at the customs counter and watched while Jan inserted his ID card in the slot.

"Welcome to Egypt," the machine said in a contralto female voice. "We hope that your visit will be an enjoyable one . . . Mr. Kulozik. Would you be so kind as to press your thumb to the plate. Thank you. You may remove your card now. There is a message for you. Will you please proceed to exit four where you will be met. Next please."

The computer dealt with Aileen just as swiftly. While the ritual welcome was being spoken it checked her identity, verifying with her thumb print that she was the person referred to on the ID card. Then making sure that the trip was an approved one.

They were met at the exit by a perspiring, sunburnt man in a tight blue uniform. "Mr. Kulozik and party? I'm from the Magna Palace, your honor. I have your bags aboard and we can leave when you are ready." His English was good, but he had an accent that Jan could not place.

"We'll go now."

The airport had been built at the water's edge and the small hovercraft sat on its pad at the end of the slipway. The driver opened the door for them and they climbed into the air-conditioned interior. There were a dozen seats, but they were the only passengers. In a moment the craft rose up on the blast of air, then drifted down to the water and out onto it, picking up speed.

"We are now going south in the Gulf of Suez," the driver said. "On your left you will see the Sinai Peninsula. Ahead, on your right, you will soon be able to see the peak of Mount Gharib which is one-thousand, seven-hundred and twenty-three meters high . . ."

"I've been here before," Jan said. "You can save the guided tour."

"Thank you, your honor."

"Jan, I wanted to hear it. I don't even know where we are?"

"Did you fail geography as well as history?"

"Don't be cruel."

"Sorry. We'll be coming out into the Red Sea soon and making a sharp left turn into the Gulf of Aqaba where the sun always shines and it is always hot, except in the summer when it is even hotter. And right in the middle of all that lovely sun and water is the Magna Palace where we are going. You aren't British, are you, driver?"

"No, your honor, South African."

"You're a long way from home."

"A continent away, sir."

"I'm thirsty," Aileen said.

"I'll get some drinks from the bar."

"I'll do that, your honor," the driver said, flicking onto automatic and jumping to his feet. "What will be your pleasure?"

"Whatever you suggest . . . I don't know your name."

"Piet, sir. There is cold beer and—"

"Just the thing. You too, Aileen?"

"Yes, thank you."

Jan drained half of the foaming glass and sighed. He was getting into the holiday mood at last. "Have one yourself, Piet."

"I will. Very kind of you, sir."

Aileen looked closely at the driver, the blond hair and reddened skin, and sensed a mystery. Though the man was polite his manners were not the rough ones of a prole's. "I hate to admit it, Piet," she said, "but I have never heard of South Africa."

"Few have," he admitted. "The city of South Africa isn't very big, just a few thousand whites in a sea of blacks. We're a fortress built over the diamond mines, nothing else. I didn't like working in the mines and there is nothing else one can do—so I got out. I like the job here and the way I can move around." A shrill bleeping sounded and he put down his glass and hurried to the controls.

It was late afternoon when Magna appeared on the horizon, just a blur where the desert sand met the ocean. The shining glass towers of the holiday complex were soon visible; bright-sailed boats dotted the sea before them.

"I know I'm going to like this," Aileen said, laughing.

The hovercraft slid up onto the beach well clear of the boats and swimmers, at the very edge of the crumbled mud huts that made up the native town. A few burnoosed Arabs were visible, but vanished from sight before the door of the craft was unlocked.

There was an open carriage waiting for them—drawn by a donkey. Aileen clapped with joy at the sight, widened her eyes at the dark-skinned, turbaned driver, and enjoyed every moment of the short ride to the hotel. The manager hurried up to hold the door for them and greet them; porters made off with their bags. Their room was spacious with a wide balcony facing the sea. A basket of fruit was waiting on the table and the manager himself opened the bottle of champagne and poured the first glassful.

"Welcome again," he said, managing to bow and pass them the glasses at the same time.

"I love it," Aileen said, kissing Jan soundly as soon as they were alone. "And I'm dying to get into that ocean out there."

"So why don't we?"

It was as good as it looked. Despite the season the water was comfortable, the sun hot on their shoulders. England and winter were a bad dream, very far away. They swam until they were tired, then went and sat beneath the tall palm trees and had a drink in the red glow of sunset. Dinner was served on the terrace and they did not bother to change. To make the evening complete a brightly glowing full moon rose above the desert.

"I just can't believe it," Aileen said. "You must have arranged the whole thing."

"I did. The moon was due to rise two hours from now but I speeded it up for you."

"Very kind of you. Jan, look, what are they doing?"

Dark shapes were moving out from the shore, changing and growing while they watched.

"Night yachting. Getting up their sails."

"Could we do it? Do you know how?"

"Of course I do!" he said with authority, trying to

remember the little he had learned about sailing on his first visit here. "Come on, I'll show you."

It was a mess, of course, and they laughed as they stumbled over the tangled ropes, and finally had to shout to the shore for aid. One of the Arab boat handlers came out in a skiff and soon put the lines to right. A light breeze had sprung up, so that with the mainsail set they were soon moving smoothly over the calm sea. Moonlight showed the way clearly; the stars burned from horizon to horizon. Jan held the tiller with one hand, the other about Aileen who leaned against him, kissed him, her skin warm against his in her brief bathing costume.

"Almost too much," she whispered.

"Never enough."

They did not tack and the wind carried them further from shore, until none of the other boats were in sight and the land had vanished in the darkness of the water.

"Aren't we too far out?" Aileen asked.

"Not really. I just thought it would be nice to be alone. I can navigate by the moon, and we can always drop sail and use the auxiliary to get back if we have to."

"I haven't the slightest idea of what you are talking about but I trust you."

A half an hour later, with the air getting cooler, Jan decided to turn around. He managed to go all aback when he tacked, but eventually the sail filled again and they could see the lights of the hotel on the horizon ahead. It was very quiet, the only sound the slight rush of water under the bow and the crackling of the sail, so that they heard the rumble of motors when they were still far away. The sound grew, quickly.

"Someone's in a hurry," Jan said, squinting into

the darkness toward the growing whine of straining engines.

"What's out there?"

"I haven't the foggiest. But we'll know soon, they seem to be coming this way. Two engines it sounds like. Funny time of night to go racing."

It happened quickly. The hammering exhausts grew louder and the first ship appeared. A dark form over a froth of white sea. Growing monstrously—aiming right at them. Aileen screamed as it loomed above them, went by them. The wake caught the boat and washed over the coaming, sending them rocking wildly.

"By God that was close," Jan gasped, holding to the cockpit edge with one hand, clasping Aileen with the other.

They had turned, looking after the first ship, so they never even saw the second one until it was too late. Jan had only a glimpse of the bow tearing down on them, crashing into their bowsprit, crushing it, capsizing them. He had only time to grab hard onto Aileen when the boat capsized.

As the water closed over his head something struck him on the leg, numbing it. The sea pulled at Aileen but he held fast, both arms about her until they surfaced again. She was sobbing and coughing as her head came above the surface and he held her up as best he could.

They were in the midst of floating debris. The yacht was gone. So were the two ships, the sound of their engines dying and vanishing.

In the middle of the dark night, in the black ocean, they were alone.

Three

At first Jan did not appreciate the complete danger of their position. Aileen was crying and coughing and it was hard enough to keep his own head above the surface as well as hers. The floating debris was black in the water around them and he pushed away from a mass of ropes, then struck a cushion with his flailing hand. It was floating high in the water and had obviously been designed for flotation use. He guided Aileen to it, pulled it under her arms. Only when he saw that she was holding fast and her head was well out of the water did he let go and look for another cushion.

"Come back!" she called out in panic.

"It's all right. I want another float for myself."

He found it easily enough and kicked his way back toward her anxious voice.

"I'm here now. It's all right."

"What's all right? We're going to die out here, drown, I know it!"

He had no easy answer because he had the terrible sensation that she was right. "They'll find us," he finally said. "The ships will come back or radio in for aid. You'll see. Meanwhile, let's kick toward shore. It's not too far."

"Which way do we go?"

That was a very good question and he was far from sure of the answer. The moon was overhead now and veiled by high clouds. And from their position, low in the water, the hotel lights were no longer visible. "This way," he said, trying to sound reassuring pushing her ahead of him.

The ships did not come back, the shore was miles away—even if they were swimming in the right direction, which he doubted very much—and he was growing cold. And tired. Aileen was only half conscious, he had the feeling that she might have struck her head when they were run down, and soon he had to stop swimming in order to hold her onto the cushion.

Could they last until morning? That was the fact he had to face. He was not going to swim ashore. What time was it? Probably not even midnight yet. And the winter nights were long. The water was not that warm. He kicked out again to get the blood flowing, to warm himself a bit. But Aileen's skin was growing colder and colder in his grasp, her breathing weaker. If she died it would be his fault, he had brought her to this place, put her life at risk. But if she died he would certainly pay for his mistake. He would not last until dawn either. And even if he did—would the searchers find them?

Dark thoughts spiraled around and around in his head and his depression was absolute. Maybe it would be easier to let go now, to drown now, put an end to everything. Yet even as the thought entered his mind he kicked out in anger, pushing them through the wet darkness. Die he might—but not by suicide. However his legs tired quickly and he stopped the futile effort and let them float downward. Holding Aileen's cold shoulders he pressed his face to hers. Was it going to end like this?

Something pushed up against his feet, and he

bent his knees in sudden terror. The thought of a creature unseen below him in the dark water was as terrifying as a nightmare. Shark? Were there sharks in this ocean? He didn't know.

It touched him again, hard from below, rising up inexorably. There was no escape. There it was, in all directions, no matter how hard he thrashed to escape.

While behind him something even blacker than the night rose up like a wall, gushing with water.

Jan struck out with his fist in pure fear—bruising his knuckles on hard metal.

Then they were out of the water, on a platform of some kind, the wind blowing coldly on his soaked skin. There was the sudden shock of recognition—then he shouted out loud.

"A submarine!"

The accident had been seen, must have been. Submarines do not rise up beneath one's feet, in the night, by accident. An infrared telescope, or perhaps the new micropulse radar. Gently, he laid Aileen on the wet planking, her head on the pillow.

"Hello there," he called out, knocking with his fist on the conning tower. Perhaps the door was on the other side. He was starting around it when a black opening suddenly appeared and men began to push their way out. One of them leaped on Aileen, stabbing her in the leg with something shining.

"What the hell do you think you're doing?" Jan shouted, jumping at them; relief turned to anger in the instant. The nearest figure turned swiftly, raising his hand with something in it, bringing it down toward Jan.

He fought back, grabbed the arm and pressed hard. The man grunted in surprise as he stabbed himself— his eyes widened with shock. He gave one immense heave, then went limp. Jan pushed him aside, whirled toward the others, fists clenched and ready. They were spread in a circle before him, bent to attack, grunting in guttural voices to one another.

"Oh, hell," one of them said, standing up straight and holding the others back with his hands. "No more fighting. We've botched this thing nicely."

"We can't stop now . . ."

"Yes we can. Get below." He turned to Jan. "You as well."

"What have you done to her?"

"Nothing important. An injection to make her sleep. We had one for you too, but poor Ota got the shot instead . . ."

"You can't force me to go."

"Don't be a fool!" the man shouted in sudden anger. "We could have left you to drown—but we surfaced to save your lives. And every moment we are exposed puts ours in danger. Stay here if you want."

He turned and followed the others through the doorway, helping pass down the unconscious Aileen. Jan hesitated only an instant, then followed. He still was not going to commit suicide.

He blinked in the fierce red glow of the compartment, figures like ruddy devils around him. For the moment he was ignored as the hatch was sealed shut, orders shouted, the deck tilted abruptly. When they were safely below the surface, the man who had spoken to him on deck turned from the periscope and waved Jan toward the door at the end of the compartment.

"Let's go to my cabin. Get some dry clothes for you, something warm to drink. The girl will be taken care of too, don't worry."

Jan sat on the edge of the neatly made bunk, glad of the warmth of the blanket about his shoulders, shivering strongly. He was handed a cup of sweet tea which he sipped at gratefully. His savior—or captor?—

sat in the chair opposite lighting his pipe. A man in his fifties, gray hair and tanned skin, dressed in a worn khaki uniform with epaulets of rank on his shoulders.

"I am Captain Tachauer," he said, blowing out a cloud of rank smoke. "Could I have your name?"

"Kulozik. Jan Kulozik. Who are you and what are you doing here? And why the attempt to knock us out?"

"It seemed a good idea at the time. No one wanted to leave you two up there to drown, though it was suggested at least once with a marked lack of enthusiasm. We are not murderers. Yet if we saved you it would reveal our presence and there could be major repercussions. Finally the sleeping shots were suggested and approved. What else could we do? But it's obvious we're not professionals at this sort of thing. Ota got his own needle and is now having a good snore for himself."

"Who are you?" Jan asked again, looking at the unfamiliar uniform, at the books in a rack on the wall printed in an alphabet he had never seen before. Captain Tachauer sighed heavily.

"Israeli Navy," he said. "Welcome aboard."

"Thank you—and thank you as well for saving our lives. I just don't understand why you were worried about us seeing you. If you are involved in security work for the UNO Navy, I'll keep my mouth shut. I have a security clearance."

"Please, Mr. Kulozik, no more." The Captain raised his hand in a stopping motion. "You speak out of ignorance of the political situation here."

"Ignorance! I'm no prole. My education contains two graduate degrees."

The Captain's eyebrows lifted in appreciation of the degrees, but he did not seem too excited by them.

22

"I'm not referring to your technical expertise, which I am sure is considerable, but to certain gaps in your knowledge of world history produced by errors of fact that are firmly implanted in your textbooks."

"I don't know what you are talking about, Captain Tachauer. We have no censorship in our education in Britain. In the Soviet States, perhaps, but not in ours. I have complete freedom of access to any book in our libraries, as well as computer printouts of as many as I wish to consult."

"Very impressive," the Captain said, not looking impressed. "I have no intention of arguing politics with you at this time of night in our present condition. I just want to tell you as an inescapable fact that the nation of Israel is not a UNO conclave of factories and farms as you have been taught in your schools. It is a free and independent nation—almost the only one left on the face of the globe. But we can keep our independence as long as we don't leave this area or make our position known to anyone other than the ruling powers of your world. That is the danger we faced when we rescued you. Your knowledge of our existence, particularly here in this body of water where we are not supposed to be, could cause us immense damage. It might even lead to the nuclear destruction of our country. Your rulers have never been happy with our existence. If they thought they could get away unscathed they would obliterate us tomorrow . . ."

The telephone buzzed and Captain Tachauer picked it up. He listened and muttered an answer.

"I'm needed," he said, standing. "Make yourself comfortable. There's more tea here in the thermos."

What on earth had he been talking about? Jan sipped the strong tea, rubbing unconsciously at the black and blue bruise that was beginning to appear on his leg. The history books can't lie. Yet this submarine was here—and acting very circumspectly—and they were obviously worried about something. He wished that he wasn't so tired, his thoughts so clogged.

"Feeling any better," the girl said, slipping through the curtains that covered the doorway, then sitting in the Captain's chair. She had blonde hair and green eyes and was very attractive. She wore a khaki blouse and shorts, her legs were tanned and smooth, and Jan drew his eyes away from them with an embarrassed start. She smiled. "My name is Sara and you are Jan Kulozik. Anything more I can get you?"

"No, no thank you. Wait, yes, some information. Do you know what those ships were doing that ran us down? I want to report them."

"I don't know."

But she added nothing else. Just sat and looked at him calmly. The silence grew until he realized that was all she was going to say.

"Aren't you going to tell me?" he asked.

"No. It's for your own good. If you reveal your knowledge at any time you will be put instantly on the security suspect list and watched. For the rest of your life. Your advancement, career, everything will be in jeopardy until the end of your days."

"I'm afraid, Sara, that you know very little about my country. We have Security, yes, in fact my brother-in-law is a rather high officer. But we don't have anything like that. For proles, perhaps, if they are known troublemakers. They must be watched. But not for someone in my position . . ."

"What exactly is your position?"

"I'm an engineer, from a good family. I have the best connections."

"I see. One of the oppressors. A slave master."

"I resent the implications of that . . ."

"I'm not implying anything, Jan. Just stating a fact. You have your kind of society and we have ours.

A democracy. Maybe it's a word you don't even know. It doesn't matter since we are probably the last democracy in the world. We rule ourselves and we are all equal. As opposed to your slaveocracy where all are born unequal, live and die that way since nothing can ever change. From your point of view I'm sure it doesn't look too bad. Since you're the one on the top. But don't rock the boat. Your personal position could change very quickly if you were under suspicion. There is vertical mobility in your culture in only one direction. Down."

Jan laughed aloud. "Nonsense."

"Do you really believe that? All right. I'll tell you about the ships. There is a brisk trade in drugs through the Red Sea. The traditional trade from the east. Heroin for the masses. Smuggled in through Egypt or Turkey. Where there is a need—and your proles have a great need for escape—there is always money and men who will supply it. None of these drugs goes through the areas we control, we see to that, which is another reason why we are suffered to exist. This submarine patrol is just one of the ways we make sure. As long as the smugglers stay away from us we ignore them. But your state security forces have patrols as well and one of these was after that smuggler that almost ran you down. It was the coast guard that hit you. We doubt if they saw you in the darkness. In any case, they did take care of the smuggler. We saw the light of the explosion, and we tracked the coast guard returning to port alone."

Jan shook his head. "I've never heard of any of this. The proles have all the bennies and joints they need . . ."

"They need far stronger drugs to numb the existence that they lead. Now, please, stop interrupting every minute to say you have never heard about any of this. I *know* that—and that is why I am trying to tell you what is happening. The world as it really is is *not* the world you have been told about. It shouldn't matter to you, in the ruling minority, fat and rich in a hungry world. But you wanted to know. So I am telling you that Israel is a free and independent country. When all of the Arabian oil ran out the world turned their back on the Near East, happy at last to be free of the burden of the rich sheikhs. But we are here permanently—and the Arabs won't go away. They tried invasion again, but without material from outside, they couldn't win. We stayed alive, just barely, a capacity we have shown before. And we did what we could to help when things got bad. When Arab populations stabilized we taught them the traditional farming crafts of this part of the world, things they had forgotten in their years of financial exuberance. By the time the rest of the world took notice of us we had the area stabilized, viable. There were fruits and vegetables for export. It was a situation they were not happy with—but one that they accepted. Particularly when we demonstrated that our nuclear rockets were as good as theirs and if they wanted to destroy us they would have to accept a good deal of destruction of their own. And that situation has continued to the present day. Perhaps our entire country is a ghetto, but we are used to living in ghettos. And within our walls we are free."

Jan started to protest again, then thought better of it and sipped at his tea. Sara nodded approvingly.

"So now you know. For your own sake don't spread the knowledge around. And for our sake I am going to ask you to do us a favor. The Captain would not ask a favor of you, but I have no such compunction. Don't tell anyone about this submarine. For your own security as well. We are going to put you ashore in a few minutes, on the beach where you could have drifted after the accident. They'll find you there. The girl knows nothing. She was apparently unconscious, concussion, when they gave her the shot. She will be all right, the doctor says that there is no danger. You will be all right too if you keep your mouth shut. Will you?"

"Yes, of course, I won't say anything. You saved our lives. But I think a lot of what you said is lies, it has to be."

"That's very nice." She reached over and patted his arm. "You think whatever you like, *ingileh*, as long as you keep your big goyish mouth shut."

Before he could muster up an answer she was out of the door and gone. The Captain did not return and no one else talked to him until he was ordered on deck. Aileen was brought up as well, with great haste, and they were paddled ashore to an invisible shore in an inflatable dinghy. The moon was behind high clouds but gave enough light to make out the beach and the desert beyond. Aileen was placed gently in the sand and the blanket pulled roughly from his shoulders. The cushion from the yacht was thrown down and then they disappeared. Being as gentle as possible, Jan pulled Aileen above the tide line; the only marks in the sand were of his own making. The dinghy and the submarine were gone, vanished and only a memory. A memory that seemed more and more unreal with every passing minute.

It was soon after sunrise that the search copter spotted them and settled down for a landing on the shore nearby.

Four

"Absolutely sound. Fit as a fiddle," the doctor said. Tapping the readout on the screen. "Look at that blood pressure—wish I had one like it. EKG, EEG, all of it just fine. Here, I'll give you a printout for your own physician, for his records." He touched the controls on the computer diagnostician and a long sheet of typing emerged.

"It's not myself I'm worrying about, it's Mrs. Pettit."

"Please don't concern yourself, my dear young man." The fat doctor patted Jan's knee with more than professional sympathy. Jan moved his leg away and looked coldly at the man. "She has had a mild concussion, swallowed a little sea water, nothing more. You can see her whenever you want to. I would like her to stay in the hospital for a day. To rest mostly, since she needs no medical care. And here is your medical readout."

"I don't want it. Have it transferred to my company's records for the physicians."

"That could be difficult."

"Why? You have a satellite link, the call can be made easily. I can pay for it if you feel it is not within the hospital's budget."

"No such thing! Of course I shall take care of it

28

instantly. Let us just, ha-ha, unplug you first." The doctor's hands moved efficiently, detaching the tell-tales from Jan's skin, slipping the needle from his vein, then dabbing his skin with alcohol.

Jan was pulling on his trousers when the door burst open and a familiar voice called out to him.

"There you are, alive and well, you had me worried."

"Smitty! What are you doing here?"

Jan took his brother-in-law's hand and pumped it enthusiastically. The great beak of a nose, the lean and hard features, were a touch of home among the rotund softness of the locals. Thurgood-Smythe seemed just as pleased to see him.

"You gave me quite a scare. I was in Italy, at a conference, when word reached me. Pulled some strings, grabbed a military jet, and was just landing when they said you had been found. I must say, you don't look any the worse for the experience."

"You should have seen me last night hanging onto the cushion with one arm and Aileen with the other—and kicking with one leg. Not something I would like to do a second time."

"It sounds quite the experience. Put on your shirt and I'll buy you a drink and you'll tell me all about it. Did you see the ship that ran you down?"

Jan had turned to get his shirt and he pushed his arms into the sleeves. All of the warnings of the night came back in a rush. Had Smitty's voice changed when he had asked that last, not-so-innocent question? He was Security after all—with enough status to commandeer a military jet in the middle of the night. Now was the moment. To tell the whole truth—or to begin to lie. He pulled the shirt over his head, his voice muffled a bit by the fabric.

"Nothing. Night black as pitch, neither ship with

a light. First one went past so close we almost capsized—the second sank us." No lies there so far. "I'd
like to find out who the bastards were. My fault for
being out there without any lights, but still . . ."

"Absolutely right, old son. Plant a rocket and I'll
help you to do it. I put a tracer out on them. Two
navy ships on maneuvers and well out of the area
where they should have been. As soon as they dock
they are going to hear a thing or two, you can be sure
of that."

"The hell with it, Smitty, it was an accident."

"You're too nice to them—but you're a gentleman.
Now let's look in on Aileen, then get that drink."

Aileen kissed them both soundly, then cried a bit,
with joy she said, and insisted on telling Thurgood-
Smythe every detail of their adventure. Jan waited,
trying not to let the tension show. Would she remember the submarine? And someone was lying; there
were two completely different stories. Smugglers and
an explosion—or two naval vessels? How could he be
sure?

". . . and—bang! Just like that we were in the
sea. I was choking and blubbering but the ancient
mariner here managed to keep my head above water.
I'm sure I tried to scratch him for his troubles. Panic!
I don't think I knew the meaning of the word before.
And my head hurt and things kept getting woozy and
going in and out of focus. Then there was a cushion to
hang onto and we were floating in the water and I
remember him trying to cheer me up and me not be-
lieving it at all. And then—nothing."

"Nothing?" Thurgood-Smythe asked.

"A blank. Next thing I knew I was in this bed and
they had to tell me what had happened." She took
Jan's hand. "And I'm never going to be able to thank
you. A girl doesn't get her life saved every day. Now
get out of here before I start crying again."

They left the hospital in silence and Thurgood-Smythe pointed to the nearest café. "In there all right?"

"Of course. Did you talk to Liz?"

"Not last night. I didn't want to wake her up and start her worrying too. There was no point in putting her through a night of trouble. But I called her this morning as soon as I heard you were safe and she sends all of her sisterly love. And says to stay out of small boats after this."

"That's Liz all right. Cheers."

They raised the glasses and drank. The brandy burned, warmed a spot within Jan that he had not known was chilled. It had been close. And it wasn't over yet. He had to fight back the desire to tell his brother-in-law everything about the night before. The submarine, the rescue, the two ships, everything. Wasn't he committing a crime by not reporting what had happened? Only one thing stopped him from blurting out the truth. The Israelis had saved his life—and Sara had said that he would be jeopardizing theirs if he talked about the submarine. Forget it. He had to forget everything.

"I'll have another one of these," he said.

"And I'll join you. Forget about last night and start enjoying your holiday."

"My thoughts exactly."

But the memory would not go away and was lurking in the corner of his mind ready to pounce whenever he relaxed. When he said good-bye to Thurgood-Symthe at the VTOL pad, there was guilty satisfaction that he would not have to be alert and remember his lies all of the time.

The sun, the food, the water, all were good—although they did not go boating again by unspoken agreement. In bed Aileen expressed her thanks for what he had done with a passion that left them both

31

happily exhausted. Yet the other memory was always there. When he awoke at dawn, her red hair against his cheek, he thought of Sara in the sub and what she had said. Was he living a lie? It didn't seem possible.

The two weeks ended and, in a way, they did not mind turning their backs on the warm waters of that sea. Some memories could be left behind there. They had good tans to show their envious friends back in England and they looked forward to it. And some good meat and potatoes after all the rich and unusual food. Good enough, but you wouldn't want to live on it forever. They parted in the air terminal at Victoria, with one last lingering kiss, and Jan went to his apartment. He made a pot of strong tea and took it to his workroom, unconsciously relaxing as he walked through the door and the lights came on. The wall over the bench was racked with instruments, their chrome surfaces polished and gleaming. The workbench was clean, with the rows of tools mounted on it. Held in a frame was the breadboarded apparatus that he had been working on before he had gone away. Jan sat down before it and rotated it—then picked up a jeweler's loupe to examine a soldered connection. It was almost ready to go—if it went at all. It should; the computer simulation had checked out. And the idea was a simple one.

All of the large ocean going vessels used satellites for navigation. There were always at least two of these satellites above the horizon anywhere on the ocean. The shipboard navigating instruments sent out a signal that was bounced back by the satellites. These signals, giving the azimuth, direction and angles of elevation of the satellites, were fed into a shipboard computer. It was simple work then for the computer to work out the ship's position in the ocean accurate within a few meters. These navigation instruments were very efficient, but also bulky and quite expensive—which did not matter at all to a large ship. But what about a small navigation instrument? For a personal yacht. Jan had been working for some time on a simplified design that would accomplish the same thing for any ship, no matter what the size. An instrument small enough and cheap enough for anyone to use. If it worked he might even patent it, make a profit. That was in the future. Meanwhile he had to get it to work—then miniaturize all of the components.

Yet he wasn't relaxing here, as he usually did. Something else was on his mind. He finished the last of the tea and took the tray into the kitchen. Then went into the library on the way back and took down volume thirteen of the Encyclopedia Britannica and flipped through the pages to the entry he wanted.

ISRAEL. Manufacturing and agricultural enclave on the shores of the Mediterranean. Former site of the Nation of Israel. Depopulated during the plague years and resettled by UNO volunteers in 2065. Now administers the Arab farmlands to the north and south and is responsible for all shipments of produce from the area.

There it was, in black and white, in a book he could trust. The facts of history shorn of all emotion. Just facts, facts . . .

That was untrue. He *had* been on that submarine, and *had* talked with the Israelis. Or some people who called themselves Israelis. Had they been? If not, who were they really? What had he got involved with?

What was it that T.H. Huxley had said? He remembered reading it when he first entered university and writing it down and posting it above his desk. It was something about the ". . . great tragedy of science—the slaying of a beautiful hypothesis by an ugly fact." He had adhered to those hard-headed words

33

and studied science in a hard-headed way. Facts, give him facts—then let the hypotheses fall by the way.

What were the facts here? He had been aboard a submarine that could not exist in the world as he understood it. But the *sub* had existed. Therefore his world image was at fault.

Saying it that way made it easier to understand—but made him angry as well. He was being lied to. The hell with the rest of the world, they could take care of themselves, but he, Jan Kulozik, was being lied to on a continuous, full-time basis. He didn't like it. But how could he find out which were the lies, which the truths? With this realization came the accompanying one that Sara was right about the danger he faced. Lies were secrets and secrets were meant to be kept. And these were state secrets. Whatever he did, whatever he discovered, he could tell no one else about it.

Where did he start? There would be full records somewhere—but he did not know which records to look for or even what he was looking for. That would take some thought, some planning. Yet there was one thing he could do at once. Look closer at the world around him. What had Sara called him? A slave master. He didn't feel like one. It was just that his class was used to taking care of things, taking care of people who couldn't take care of themselves. And the proles certainly couldn't be allowed to be in charge or everything would come to pieces. They just weren't bright enough or responsible enough. That was the natural order of things.

They were there at the bottom, the proles, the millions and millions of unwashed bodies—most of whom were on the dole. Where they had been ever since the Wreckers let the world go to rack and ruin. It was all there in the history books. If they were all alive today it was no thanks to themselves or the Wreckers who had let it happen, but was due to the hard work of the people of his class who had taken up the reins of government. Executives and engineers who had made the most of the world's shrinking resources. The hereditary members of Parliament had less and less to do with the matters of running a technological society. The Queen was just a figurehead. Knowledge was king and knowledge had kept the world alive. It had been touch and go for a while—but mankind had survived. The satellite stations had alleviated the energy crisis when the oil supplies had finally run out, and fusion power had eventually brought security to the world.

But the lesson had been learned; the fragile ecology of a single world could be easily unbalanced. Resources ran out, raw materials were needed. The first step was to the moon, then the asteroid belt where elements were to be had for the taking. Then the stars. Hugo Foscolo made that possible, with his discovery of what had come to be known as the Foscolo Discontinuity. Foscolo had been a theoretical mathematician, an unnoticed genius who earned his living as a school teacher in the state of Sao Paulo, Brazil, in a city with the impossible name of Pindamonhangaba. The discontinuity was in the theory of relativity and when he published, in an obscure mathematical journal, Foscolo had apologized for casting doubt on the accepted theories of a great man and asked humbly that qualified mathematicians and physicists point out the error in his equations.

They could not—and a space drive was born that took men to the stars. It took only a hundred years to search and settle and spread through the nearest star systems. It was a glorious history and it had to be a true history because it existed.

There were no slaves, Jan knew that, and was angry at Sara for saying it. There was peace in the world, and justice, food enough for all, and each man

35

to his station. What was that word she had used? Democracy. A form of government, obviously. He had never heard of it. Back to the encyclopedia—only with a certain reluctance this time. Jan did not enjoy finding an error in those thick tomes. It was like discovering that a treasured painting was in reality a fake. He took the volume down and walked over to the high windows to catch the light.

> DEMOCRACY. An archaic historical political science term for that form of government which flourished briefly in the small city-states of Greece. According to Aristotle, democracy is the perverted form of the third form of government . . .

There was more like this and all just about as interesting. Some historical kind of government, like cannibalism, that had come and gone. What had this to do with the Israelis? It was all a little puzzling. Jan looked out of the window at the gray sky and the ice-specked surface of the Thames below. He shivered, still feeling the tropic sun in his bones. Where did he begin?

Not with history. It was not his field; he had no idea where to look. Did he really have to look at all? In truth he didn't want to, and he had the sudden dark sensation that once he started this quest there would be no turning back. Once Pandora's box was opened it could never be closed again. Did he want to find out these things? Yes! She had called him a slave master—and he knew he was not. Even a prole would laugh at the suggestion.

That was it. The proles. He knew enough of them, he worked with them, that was where he would start. He would go back to the Walsoken Plant in the morning—he was expected there in any case to check on the installation and maintenance that he had ordered. Only this time he would talk more to the proles there. Admittedly he had not done this very much in the past, but that was only because he had been busy. As long as he was circumspect he would not get into trouble. There were certain social customs about dealing with proles and he was not going to break them. But he was going to ask some questions and listen closely to the answers.

It did not take him long to discover that this was not an easy thing to do.

"Welcome back, your honor, welcome back," the manager said, hurrying from the works door when Jan pulled up in his car. His breath smoked in the cold air and he moved uneasily from one foot to the other.

"Thank you, Radcliffe. I hope things have been going along well while I have been away?"

Radcliffe's ready smile had an edge of worry to it. "Not bad at all, sir. Not completed, I'm sorry to say, shortage of spares. Perhaps you can help us expedite them. But let me show you the record."

Nothing appeared to have changed. There were still pools of liquid underfoot despite the lethargic actions of a man with a mop. Jan started to snap about this—actually opened his mouth—then closed it again. Radcliffe seemed to be expecting it too because he glanced quickly over his shoulder. Jan smiled back. One for the home team. Perhaps he had been quick to find fault in the past—but he wasn't going to do that now. You do more catching with honey. A few pleasant words and then a conversation. It was working well.

It still took an effort to control his temper when he went through the printouts. He had to say something.

"Really, Radcliffe, I don't mean to be repetitive—

but this won't do at all. You've had over two weeks and the list is as long as ever."

"We've had men out sick, sir, a hard winter. And you'll see, this work has been done . . ."

"But you've had breakdowns that more than make up for it . . ."

Jan heard the angry tone in his voice and snapped his mouth shut. He was not going to lose his temper this time. Trying not to stamp he went to the office door and looked out at the main floor of the plant. A movement caught his eye and he saw the tea trolley being pushed down a corridor. Yes, a cup of tea, that was more like it. He went to his case and opened it.

"Blast!"

"Anything wrong, sir?"

"Nothing important. Just that when I left my bag at the hotel this morning I forgot to pick up my thermos of tea."

"I can send a man on a bike, sir. Won't be but a few minutes."

"No, not worth the effort." Then Jan had the tremendous, almost daring idea. "Get the trolley in here. We'll both have a cup of tea."

Radcliffe's eyes opened wide and he was silent for a moment with shock. "Oh, no, your honor. You wouldn't like the stuff we serve here. Right muck. I'll send . . ."

"Nonsense. Get it in here."

It was a trial by embarrassment that Jan never noticed as he went through the printouts again, checking off priorities. The bent tea woman kept rubbing her hands on her skirt and bowing slightly in his direction. Radcliffe slipped out and returned quickly with a clean towel with which she wiped and wiped one of the mugs. When it was finally served it rested alone on the battered tray.

"You too, Radcliffe, that's an order."

The tea was hot and that was about all that could be said for it, the mug thick and chipped where he put it to his lips. "Very good," Jan said.

"Yes, your honor, it is." Agonized eyes above his own cup.

"We'll have to do this again."

The answer was silence and Jan had no idea where to take the conversation from there. The silence lengthened until he had finished his tea and there was nothing to do except go back to work.

There was more than enough calibration to do, as well as some pressing repairs that had been ignored during his absence. Jan became involved in his labors and it was well after six before he yawned and stretched and realized that the day shift had all gone home. He remembered Radcliffe looking in and saying something, but that was all. That was enough for one day. He packed his papers, slipped into the fleece-lined coat, and let himself out. The night was cold and dry, the stars flickering icily above. A long way from the Red Sea. It was a relief to get into the car and turn on the heater.

A good day's work. The control setup was working fine and if he applied pressure the repairs and maintenance might be improved. *Had* to be improved. He pulled hard on the wheel to avoid a bicyclist who suddenly appeared in the beam of his headlights. Dark clothes and a black bike with no reflectors. Wouldn't they ever learn? Empty fields on all sides and not a house in sight. What on earth was the man doing out here in the darkness?

The next turn brought the answer. Glowing windows and a lighted sign beside the road ahead. A public house, of course, he had passed it countless times without even noticing it. No reason to. Jan slowed the car. *The Iron Duke* the board read, with a

39

portrait of the Duke himself, aristocratic nose held high. But not so aristocratic, the clientele; not a car about and bicycles racked along the front wall. No wonder he had never noticed it before.

He hit the brakes. Of course! He would stop here for a drink, talk to people. There could be nothing wrong with this. The customers would surely be pleased to have him. Bring a touch of interest to a cold evening. What a very good idea.

Jan closed and locked the car and stamped across the hard ground to the front door. It swung wide at his touch and he entered a large, brightly lit room, the air thick with the clouds of cheap tobacco and marijuana smoke. A loud, very boring piece of music was pouring from wall speakers and drowned out any sound of conversation from the crowd of men at the bar, seated at the small tables. No women, he noticed with interest. In a proper pub at least half—or more— of the customers would be women. He found an opening at the bar and rapped for attention when the barman did not notice him.

"Why yes, sir, very pleased to have you here, sir," the man said, hurrying over with a warm smile on his fat lips. "What will be your pleasure?"

"A large whiskey—and something for yourself as well."

"Why thank you, sir. I'll have similar."

Jan didn't notice the brand name; it was rougher than the whiskey he usually drank. But fairly priced. The round was less than a single at his local. These people had no cause for complaint.

There was more space at the bar now—in fact he had it almost to himself. Jan turned about and there, at a nearby table, sat Radcliffe and some of the other workers from the Walsoken Plant. Jan waved and walked over.

"Well, Radcliffe, relaxing a bit?"

"You might say so, your honor." The words were cold and formal; the man seemed embarrassed for some reason.

"Mind if I join you?"

There were some wordless mutters that Jan took to be assent. He pulled an empty stool over from the next table and sat down and looked around. No one met his eyes; they all seemed to be finding things of interest in their liters of beer.

"Cold night, isn't it?" One of them drank noisily, the only answer. "And the winters are going to stay cold for the next few years. It's called a little climatic, a small weather change within the larger cycles of weather. We won't have another ice age, not at once, but we can count on these cold winters lasting awhile."

His audience was not exactly bursting with enthusiasm and Jan had the sudden realization that he was making a fool of himself. Why had he come in here in the first place? What could he learn from these stolid dolts? The whole idea was stupid. He drained his glass and left it on the table.

"Enjoy yourself, Radcliffe. All of you. See you at work in the morning and we'll really get cracking on the maintenance. A lot of work to do."

They muttered something which he didn't stay to hear. The devil with theories and blond-haired girls in submarines. He must be going out of his head to do what he was doing, think what he was thinking. The hell with it. The bite of cold air was sharp and good after the reek of the pub. His car was there with two men bent over the open door.

"Stop there! What do you think you're doing?"

Jan ran toward them, slipping on the icy ground. They looked up quickly, a blur of white faces, then turned and ran into the darkness.

"Stop! Do you hear me—stop!"

Breaking into his car, criminals! They weren't getting away with it. He ran after them around the building and one of them stopped. Good! Turned to him . . .

He never saw the man's fist. Just felt the explosion of agony on his jaw. Falling.

It was a hard, cruel blow, and he must have been unconscious for a moment or two because the next thing he knew he was on his hands and knees, shaking his head with pain. There were shouts around him, more running footsteps, and hands on his shoulders pulling him to his feet. Someone helped him to walk back to the pub, into a small room where he dropped heavily into a deep chair. There was a wet towel then, cool on his forehead, stinging on his jaw. He took it and held it himself and looked up at Radcliffe who was alone in the room with him.

"I know the man, the man that hit me," Jan said.

"I don't think you do, sir. I don't think it was no one who works at the plant. I have someone watching the car, sir. Nothing taken that I can see, you were too quick. Looks like a little damage where the door was jimmied open . . ."

"I said I *know* him. Had a clear view of his face when he hit me. And he did work at the plant!"

The cool cloth helped. "Sampson, something like that. Remember, the man who tried to burn the place down. Simmons—that's the name."

"Couldn't have been him, sir. He's dead."

"Dead? I don't understand. He was in perfect health two weeks ago."

"Killed himself, sir. Couldn't face going back on the dole. Studied for years to get the job. Only had it a few months."

"Well you can't blame me for his incompetence. You agreed with me, as I recall, that firing him was the only thing to do. You remember?"

Radcliffe did not lower his eyes this time and there was an unaccustomed note of hardness in his voice.

"I remember asking you to keep him on. You refused."

"You aren't implying by any chance that I'm responsible for his death, are you?"

Radcliffe did not answer, nor did his empty expression change. Nor did he lower his eyes from Jan's. It was Jan who turned away first.

"Management decisions are hard to make sometimes. But they have to be done. Yet I swear that man was Simmons. Looked just like him."

"Yes, sir. It was his brother. You can find that out easy enough if you want to."

"Well thank you for telling me. The police will deal with this matter easily enough."

"Will they, Engineer Kulozik?" Radcliffe sat up straight and there was a timbre in his voice that Jan had never detected before. "Do you have to tell them? Simmons is dead, isn't that enough? His brother is looking after the wife and kiddies. All on the dole. For all of their lives. Do you wonder he was angry? I'm not excusing him; he had no business doing what he did. If you would forget it there would be some grateful people around here. He hasn't been the same since he found his brother dead."

"I have a duty . . ."

"Do you, sir? To do what? To stay with your own kind and leave us alone. If you hadn't come nosing around here tonight, pushing in where you're not wanted, none of this would have happened. Leave well enough alone, I say. Get in your car and get out of here. Leave things as they are."

"Not wanted . . . ?" Jan tried to accept the thought, that these men could feel that way about him.

"Not wanted here. I've said enough, your honor. Maybe too much. Do whatever you want. What's done is done. Someone will be by the car until you're ready to go."

He left Jan alone. Feeling more alone than he had at any other time in his life.

Five

Jan drove slowly back to his hotel in Wisbech in a poisonous frame of mind. There was a crowd in the bar at the White Lion which he passed by swiftly and on up the creaking stairs to his room. The bruise on the side of his face felt far worse than it looked. He bathed it again in cold water, holding the damp cloth to his face and staring at himself in the mirror. He felt an absolute fool.

After pouring himself a large drink from the room bar, he stared unseeingly out of the window and tried to understand why he had not yet called the police. With every passing minute it was becoming more and more impossible, since they would want to know why he had delayed. Why was he delaying? He had been brutally attacked, his car broken into, damaged. He had every right to report the man.

Had he been responsible for Simmons's death?

He couldn't be, it was not possible. If a man did not do his job well, he did not deserve to have it. When one man in ten had employment he had better be good or he was out. And Simmons had been no good. So he was out. And dead.

"I did not do it," Jan said aloud, firmly. Then went to pack his bag. The hell with the Walsoken Plant and all the people who worked there. His responsibility had ended when the control installation had been completed and come on line. Maintenance was not his job. Someone else could worry about that. He would send in his report in the morning and let engineerconcent worry about what to do next. There was plenty of work waiting for him; with his seniority he could pick and choose. And he did not choose to stay on at the leaking spirit works among the frozen fields.

His face hurt and he drank more than he should on the trip back. When the car reached the London exit of the highway he switched onto manual control with no result. The computer had been monitoring his blood alcohol level and he was over the legal minimum. It did not relinquish control. The drive was slow, dull, and infuriating since the computer had only a few routes through London and all were out of the way for him. No short cuts. And hesitancy at all crossings, with priority given to any manually operated vehicle no matter how slow. The computer only cut out at the garage door and he exacted a small amount of pleasure from speeding headlong down the ramp and slamming into his space with a fender-scratching crunch. More whiskey followed and he woke at three in the morning to find the light still on and the TV talking to itself in the corner. After that he slept late and was just finishing his first cup of coffee when the door annunciator signaled. He squinted at the screen and pressed the release. It was his brother-in-law.

"You look a little on the ragged side this morning," Thurgood-Smythe said, laying his coat and gloves neatly on the couch.

"Coffee?"

"Please."

"I feel like I look," Jan said, having already fixed on the lie when he awoke. "Slipped on the ice, think I loosened a tooth. Came home and drank too much to numb the pain. Damn car wouldn't even let me drive."

"The curse of automation. Have it looked at yet?"

"No. No need. Just a bruise. I feel the fool."

"Happens to the best of us. Elizabeth wants you over to dinner tonight, can you come?"

"Anytime. Best cook in London. As long as it is not one of her matchmaking sessions." He looked suspiciously at Thurgood-Smythe who pointed a finger and smiled.

"Just what I told her and although she protested that the girl was one in a million, she finally agreed not to have her. Three for dinner."

"Thanks, Smitty. Liz won't face the fact that I'm not the marrying kind."

"I told her that you will probably be sowing wild oats on your deathbed and she thought I was being vulgar."

"I only hope that it will be true. But you didn't come all the way across the city when a call would have done as well."

"Of course not. Got another gadget for you to look at." He took a flat package out of his pocket and passed it over.

"I don't know how well my eyes will focus today. But I'll give it a try."

Jan slipped a metal case out of the envelope and opened it. There were a number of tiny readouts and controls inside. It was beautifully made. Thurgood-Smythe had brought other extracurricular work to Jan in the past. Electronic instruments that Security was testing, or technical problems that needed expert advice. It was in the family and Jan had always been glad to help. Particularly when there was a cash bonus if he had to devote any time to the work.

"It looks very nice," he said. "But I haven't the slightest idea of what it does."

"Wiretap detection."

"Impossible."

"That's what everyone thinks, but we have some original people in the lab. This device is so sensitive that it analyzes every element of a circuit for basic resistance and loss of strength. Apparently if you eavesdrop on a wired signal the act of detection causes a measurable alteration of the signal which in turn can be detected. Does this make any sense to you?"

"A lot. But there are so many random losses in a transmitted message, through switches, connections and such that I don't see how this thing could possibly operate."

"It's supposed to analyze every loss, find out what it is, see what its true value should be, and if it is correct go on to the next interruption of signal."

"All I can say is *wow*. If they can pack that much circuitry and control into something this big then your boys know what they are doing. What do you want from me?"

"How do we test it outside the lab to see if it works?"

"Simple enough. Put it on a lot of phones, yours and some other people in your shop, and run it for a while. Then put taps on the lines and see if it does its job."

"Sounds simple enough. They said that all you have to do is use it with the microphone input. Any problems?"

"None. Like this." Jan went to his phone and fixed the device over the microphone. The *ready* light came on. "You just talk into the mike it has as you would normally."

"Let's try it. I'll tell Elizabeth you'll be coming tonight."

It was a brief call and they both watched the rapid signals flashing from the VDU. It seemed to be doing its job. Thurgood-Smythe broke the connection and the random flickering stopped. The readout lit up.

TAP ON THIS LINE IN EXCHANGE.

"It seems to be working," Thurgood Smythe said mildly, looking at Jan.

"Working . . . Do you think it found a tap on my phone? Why on earth . . ." He thought for a moment, then pointed an accusing finger. "Out with it, Smitty. It was no accident you came today and hooked that thing up there. You knew that my line was tapped. But why?"

"Let's say I 'expected' something, Jan. I couldn't be sure." He walked to the window and looked out, tapping his hands together behind his back. "My business is full of uncertainties and suspicions. I had hints that you were under surveillance from a certain department, but I couldn't very well ask or they would have denied everything." He turned about and his face was very cold. "But now I *know* and a head or two will roll. I will not have routine-minded blockheads interfering with my family. This will be all taken care of and I wish you would forget about it."

"I would love to, Smitty. But I'm afraid I can't. I'll have to know what is going on."

"I thought you would." He raised his hand in resignation. "You were just in the wrong spot at the wrong time. That can be enough to cause these low-level bureaucrats to swing into action."

"I haven't been any place unusual—other than the ship accident."

"That's it. I wasn't exactly truthful with you

49

about what you saw. I'll tell you more, but it can't leave this room."

"You know better than to ask."

"Sorry. Been one of those weeks. Those were criminals, smugglers, in the first boat. Running drugs. The second ship was our guard. Caught them and blew them out of the water."

"Illegal drugs? I didn't know there were such things. But if there are and they caught the people— why it sounds a good item for the evening news."

"I agree with you—but others don't. They feel that publicity would only encourage law-breaking. That's policy and we're stuck with it, and you're caught in the middle. But not for long. Just forget the tap and what I have told you and be there for drinks at eight."

Jan reached out and took his brother-in-law's hand.

"If I don't sound grateful it's only because of the hangover. Thanks. It's nice to know you're there. I don't understand half of what you told me and maybe I don't want to."

"That's wisest. See you tonight."

When the door had closed, Jan poured his cup of cold coffee into the sink and went to the bar. Hair of the dog was something he usually avoided, but not today. Had Smitty been acting, or was his story true? Was there more to the story than what he had been told? The only thing he could do was act as though it were. And watch what he said on the phone.

Then came the sudden realization that what Sarah had told him on the submarine was true. The world was proving not to be the simple place he had always thought it to be.

It was snowing outside and the city of London had vanished behind a shifting curtain of white. What was to be done? He knew he was at a turning point, a branching in the road of his life. Perhaps the major branch, the one of most importance. There had been a number of shocks administered in the last weeks, more perhaps than he had experienced before in his entire lifetime. Fights in prep school, canings, exams in university, love affairs—all that had really been simple. Life had flowed toward him and he had taken it as it came. All of the decisions had been easy ones to make because they moved with the stream. Yes, this was different; this was the big one.

He could do nothing, of course, ignore everything he had heard and discovered and lead the life he had always led.

No—he couldn't possibly do that. It had all changed. The world he had lived in was not the real one, his view of reality not a true one. Israel, smugglers, submarines, democracy, slaveocracy. They were there and he had not known about them. He had been as misled as the pre-Copernicans who thought that the sun rotated around the Earth. They had believed—no, they had *known*—that it did. And they had been wrong. He had known about his world—and had been just as wrong.

At that moment he had no idea where it would lead, and had the sudden depressing feeling that it might end in disaster. It might—but the chance had to be taken. He prided himself on the freedom of his thought, the ability for rational and unemotional thinking that led him to the truth, whatever it might be.

Well there was plenty of truth in the world he knew nothing about—and he was going to find it. And he knew just how to go about it. It would be simple, it might leave traces, but if he worked it right he would not be caught.

Smiling, he sat down with a pad and a pen and began to draw a flow chart of a computer program for theft.

Six

"I can't tell you how pleased I am that you have decided to join our program," Sonia Amariglio said. "Almost all of our microcircuits are antiques fit only for museums and I despair daily of ever having anything done about them." She was gray-haired and plump, almost lost behind the big desk. And her Belgian French accent was still pronounced—her "them" sounded more like "zem"—even after her years in London. She looked like a concierge or a tired housewife. She was considered to be the top communications engineer in the entire world.

"It is my pleasure to be here, Madame Amariglio. I must admit that my motives are very selfish for joining your program."

"More selfishness of this order I do need!"

"No, it's the truth. I'm working on a smaller version of the nautical navigator and I'm having problems. I realized, finally, that my biggest problem was I knew very little about the circuitry at the satellite end. When I heard that you were looking for a microcircuit engineer I jumped at the chance."

"You are a most marvelous man and you are doubly welcome. We go to your laboratory now."

"Aren't you going to tell me what my job is first?"

"Your job is everything," she said, moving her

hands outward in a quick, all-encompassing gesture. "I want you first to understand our circuitry, ask questions, learn about our satellites. We have difficulties enough that I won't bother you with at the present. When you know your way around I will present you with a stack—so high!—of these problems. You will be sorry you ever came."

"Hardly. I really am looking forward to it."

This was the truth. He needed to work in a very large lab, and the discovery of the opening in the satellite program had been fortuitous. He really could work on the development of his navigator. And he would be of value here if the microcircuitry was as dated as he had been led to understand.

It was worse. The first satellite he examined in any detail was a great two-ton geosynchronous machine that hung in the sky 35,924 kilometers over the Atlantic Ocean. It had been in trouble for years, less than half of its circuits were still in operation, and a replacement was being manufactured. Jan was scanning through the diagrams of the replacement, with an overall schematic displayed on one screen and detailed breakdowns being shown in color on the larger screen before him. Some of the circuitry looked familiar—too familiar. He touched the prod to the screen and signaled for information. A third VDU lit up with a display of specification numbers.

"I can't believe it!" Jan said aloud.

"Did you call, your honor?" A lab assistant pushing an instrument-laden wagon stopped, turning toward him.

"No, nothing. Thank you. Just talking to myself."

The man hurried away. Jan shook his head in wonder. They had had this circuitry in his textbooks when he was in school; it must be fifty years old at least. There had been a dozen advances in the state of the art since its time. If there were more like this he could improve satellite construction easily enough by simply updating existing designs. Boring but easy. Which would give him enough free time for his personal project.

It was coming along well. He had already bypassed most of the seals on the Oxford University computer and was now searching for barred areas in the history sections. His years of computer circuit design were not being wasted.

Computers are completely unintelligent. Just big adding machines that count on their fingers. Except they have an incredible amount of fingers and can count awfully fast. They cannot think for themselves or do anything that they have not been programmed to do. When a computer functions as a memory store it answers any questions asked of it. The memory banks of a public library are open to anyone with access to a terminal. A library computer is very helpful. It will find a book by title, by author's name, or even by subject. It will supply information about a book or books until the customer is satisfied that this is indeed the book he really wants. Upon a signal the library computer will transmit the book—in a few seconds—to the memory bank of the questioning computer terminal. Simple.

But even a library computer has certain restrictions about releasing material. One is the age of the questioner and access to the pornography section. Every customer code contains the date of birth of the customer—as well as other relevant information—and if a boy age ten wants to read *Fanny Hill* he will find his request politely refused. And if he persists he will discover that the computer is programmed to inform his physician of this continuing unhealthy act.

However if the boy uses his father's identification number the computer will supply *Fanny Hill*, in the color-illustrated edition, and no questions asked.

Jan knew just how unthinking computers really were, knew as well how to get around the blocks and warnings built into their programs. After less than a week's work he had gained access to an unused terminal in Balliol College, had assigned it a new priority code, and was using it to gain access to the records he wanted to see. Even if his pryings did tip off alarms the request would only be traced back to Balliol, where things like this were expected to happen. If traced further still the circuit went through the pathology laboratory in Edinburgh before reaching his own terminal. He had installed enough alarms of his own in the program to let him know long before if he were being traced, to give him enough time to break the connection and remove all evidence of his tampering.

Today would be the major test to see if all this work had been worth the effort. He had prepared the program of requests at home and had it with him now. The morning tea break was on and most of the lab workers were away from their positions. Jan had diagrams displayed on four screens. And he was unobserved. He took out a small cigar—part of this ruse involved his taking up smoking again after a gap of almost eight years—then extracted the glow lighter from his pocket to light it with. The element went white hot in an instant and he puffed out a cloud of smoke. And put the lighter on the bench before him. Centered over the apparently accidental ink mark on the surface, that in reality had been very carefully positioned.

He cleared the small screen closest to him and asked it if it was ready to read information. It was—which meant the lighter was in the correct position over the wires in the bench. He hit the return key and the screen said *ready*. The program was now in the computer. The lighter went back into his pocket, along with the 64K magnetic bubble memory he had built inside it, in the space left when he had replaced the large battery with the smaller one.

The moment of truth. If he had written the program well it should extract the information he needed without leaving any trace of his request. Even if the alarms did go off he was sure they couldn't track him easily. For as soon as the Edinburgh computer had the information it would transmit it to Balliol. Then, without waiting for verification of receipt, it would wipe all of its memories clean of the program, the request, the transmission, and the address. Balliol would do the same as soon as it had passed on the information to him in the lab. If the information were not transmitted correctly it would mean laboriously building up the sequence of circuits again. It would be worth the effort. No effort was too large if it prevented his being traced.

Jan shook the ash from his cigar into the ashtray and saw that no one was even looking in his direction; no one could possibly see what he was doing. His actions were completely normal. He typed the code word ISRAEL onto the screen. Then typed RUN and hit the return key.

Seconds moved by. Slowly. Five, ten, fifteen. He knew that it would take time to get through to the memory, to penetrate the coded blocks, to seek out the right reference, and then to transmit it. Through tests he had run with nonclassified material from the same source he had found that eighteen seconds was the maximum time he had ever had to wait. He was allowing twenty seconds this time and no more. Now his finger was poised over the switch that would break the connection. Eighteen seconds. Nineteen.

He was about to bring it down when the screen cleared and read PROGRAM COMPLETE.

Perhaps he had something—and perhaps he

didn't. But he was not going to take a chance to find out now. Grinding out the half-smoked cigar he took a fresh one from the package and lit it. And placed the lighter on the bench. It was in the right position.

It took only a few seconds to transfer the contents of the computer's memory to the bubble memory in the lighter. Once it was safely back in his pocket he cleared all traces of what he had done from the terminal's memory, put a diagram back on the screen, and went to get his tea.

Jan did not want to do anything out of the ordinary this day so he immersed himself in the satellite studies. Once it had captured his attention he forgot all about the contents of the lighter in the intricacy of the circuit design. At the end of the day he was not the first one to leave—nor the last. In the security of his own apartment he threw down his coat and locked the door. And checked the burglar alarms he had installed. The answer was negative and it appeared that no one had been in the apartment since he had left.

The memory dumped from the core in the lighter into his computer. There was something there all right, but there was only one way to find out if his plan had succeeded. He typed RUN and hit return.

It *was* there. Pages and pages of it. The history of the State of Israel from biblical times to the present. With no gaps or fictitious accounts of UN enclaves. And it appeared to be just as Sara had told him, though in greater detail. The point of view was certainly different, but essentially what she had told him was the truth. Which made it fairly certain that everything else she had said was true as well. Was he a slave master? It would take more digging to find out what she meant by that remark and about democracy. Meanwhile he read with growing interest a history that was completely different from the one he had learned in school.

But it was not complete. In fact the record broke off suddenly in mid-line. Could this have been an accident? A glitch somewhere in the complex program that he had set up? It could be—but he did not think so. In fact he had better consider it as deliberate and rethink his whole plan. If he had missed some keying code in his gaining access to the information an alarm could have been sounded. The running program would have been cut in just this way. And traced.

There was a cold chill on the back of his neck, even though the room was warm. Now he was being foolish; the Security forces could not be that efficient. Yet—why shouldn't they be? It was always a strong possibility. He shrugged off the thought for the moment and went and took dinner from the deep freeze and put it into the microwave.

After eating he read through the material again, turning back quickly when he came to the truncated end. After that he scrolled through one more time, stopping to read the more relevant parts, then typed SCR, and cleared it all away, returning intelligence to random electrons at the touch of a button. And the lighter memory as well. He passed the lighter through the strong magnetic field of the eraser—then stopped. Not good enough. It took only a few minutes to remove the bubble memory from the lighter and drop it into his spare parts box. The original battery went back in and all evidence was removed. It might be stupid, but he felt relieved after it was done.

On the way to the lab in the morning he passed the library, usually deserted at this time of day, and a familiar voice called out to him.

"Jan, you're being the early bird."

His brother-in-law waved casually from the doorway.

"Smitty! What on earth are you doing here? Didn't know you cared about satellites."

"I care about everything. Give me a moment, will you. Come in and close the door."

"We're being mysterious this morning. Did you come to hear my discovery that we are still building satellites with circuitry dating back to the last century?"

"Wouldn't surprise me in the slightest."

"But that's not why you are here, is it?"

Thurgood-Smythe shook his head, expression as gloomy as a hound dog. "No. It's more serious than that. There's some hanky-panky going on here and I prefer to have you out of the way while we track it down."

"Hanky-panky? Is that all you're going to tell me?"

"For the moment. Elizabeth has another girl she wants to hurl at your head. This one's an heiress, which she thinks might attract you."

"Poor Liz. She never stops trying. Tell her that I'm really a homosexual and have finally come out of the closet."

"She would start finding you boys."

"You're right, you know. As soon as mother died she began trying to take care of me. I suppose she will never stop."

"Excuse me," Thurgood-Smythe said as his radio buzzed. He took it out of his pocket and listened for a moment before he spoke. "That's good. Bring the tape and the photos here."

A few moments later there was a discreet knock at the door. Thurgood-Smythe opened it just enough to get his hand through; Jan never saw who was on the other side. He sat down and rummaged through the envelope he had been given.

"Know this man?" he asked, passing over a color photograph. Jan nodded.

"I've seen him around, just to say hello to

though. Other end of the lab from me. Don't know his name."

"We do. And we're keeping an eye on him."

"Why?"

"He has just been observed using the laboratory computer for access to the commercial channels. He taped a complete performance of *Tosca*."

"So he likes opera—is that a crime?"

"No. But illicit recording is."

"You can't tell me you're worried about the few pounds fee coming out of the lab's pocket, not his?"

"Hardly. But there is a far more serious matter of unauthorized access to classified material. We have traced the signal to one of the computers in this laboratory, but couldn't pin it down any closer. We have now."

Jan felt suddenly very, very cold. Thurgood-Smythe had his head lowered, his attention on the cigarette case he had taken from his pocket, taking out a cigarette. He would have noticed something if he had been looking.

"We have no real evidence, of course," he said, closing the case. "But this man is now high on our suspect list and will be watched closely. One slip now and we have him. Thanks."

He inhaled deeply as Jan held out his glow lighter and lit the cigarette.

Seven

The pavement along the Embankment had been swept clear, but there were still white mounds up against the wall and snowy circles around the trees. Floes of ice moved swiftly on the black surface of the Thames. Jan walked through the early evening darkness, from pool of light to pool of light, head down and hands jammed into pockets, unaware of the sharp cold and needing the solitude. Ever since that morning he had looked forward to being alone, to ordering his thoughts, to checking the flow of emotions that possessed him.

Time had passed begrudgingly this day. The research had not gone well because, for the very first time, he could not bury himself in his work. The diagrams did not make sense and he went through them time and time again with the same results. Yet the hours had passed and, to his knowledge, he had done nothing suspicious. Not that he had to worry; suspicion of guilt had already been fixed on the wrong man.

Until he had seen Thurgood-Smythe in the library he had not appreciated the force of the Security procedures. He liked his brother-in-law and helped him when he could, all of the time with the knowledge that his work had something to do with Security,

61

but the reality of what Security did was far removed from normal existence. No more. The first lightning bolt had hit very close to home. Despite the cold bite of the north wind Jan could feel a filming of perspiration on his face. Damn, but Security was good! Too good. He had never expected efficiency of this kind.

It had taken skill and knowledge on his part to get through the blocks that concealed the computer memory he had wanted. But he realized now that these barriers had been there only to prevent accidental and casual access to the information. It would take a determined and resourceful person to get past them—and their only function was to make sure that this was not done easily. Once passed, a greater danger lay in wait. National secrets were meant to be kept secret. The instant he had penetrated to that information the trap had been closed, his signal detected, recorded, traced. All of his elaborate safeguards had been instantly penetrated. The thought was a frightening one. It meant that *all* of the communication lines in the country, public and private, were being monitored and controlled by the Security forces. Their powers appeared to be limitless. They could hear any conversation, tap any computer memory. Constant monitoring of all phone calls was of course physically impossible. Or was it? Monitoring programs could be written that would listen for certain words and phrases and record anything that contained them. The possible scope of the surveillance was frightening.

Why should they do all this? They had changed history—altered the true story of the world—and could monitor the world's citizens. Who were *they*? The overall answer appeared obvious when phrased that way. There were a few people at the top of society and a lot at the bottom. The ones on top wanted to stay there. And he was one of the ones on top so, unknown to him, this was all being done to make sure he kept his status unchanged. So all he had to do to keep his privileged position was absolutely nothing. Forget what he had heard, what he had uncovered, and the world would be the same.

For him. And what about the others? He had never thought about the proles much before this. They were everywhere and nowhere. Always present, always unseen. He had accepted their role in life as he had always accepted his own; something there and unchanging. What must it be like to be one? What if *he* were one?

Jan shivered. The cold, it was getting to him. Just the cold. There was the laser hologram sign of an all-night store up ahead and he hurried toward it; the door opened as he approached and admitted him to the welcoming warmth. There were some things he needed for the kitchen. He would buy them now and take his mind away from the morbidity of his thoughts. The next service number was seventeen, and it changed to eighteen when he touched the plate. Milk, he was sure he needed some of that. He typed seventeen on the number pad under the display liter of milk, then one. Butter, yes, he was low on that too.

And oranges, firm and ripe. With the word Jaffa bold on each of them, flown in fresh from summer to northern winter. He turned quickly away and hurried to the checkout.

"Seventeen," he said to the girl at the counter and she typed in the number. "Four pounds ten, sir. Do you want them delivered?"

Jan handed over his credit card and nodded. She inserted it into the machine, then returned it to him. His purchases appeared in a basket and she redirected it back inside for delivery.

"Been a cold day," Jan said. "Quite a wind blowing."

She opened her mouth slightly, then turned away when she caught his glance. She had heard his accent, seen his clothes; there could be no casual conversation between them. The girl was aware of that even if Jan wasn't. He pushed out into the night, glad of the cold bite of air on his glowing cheeks.

Back in the apartment he realized that he had no appetite at all. He eyed the whiskey bottle, but that would not be a satisfactory answer. In the end he compromised with a bottle of beer, dialed up a Bach string quartet, and wondered just what the hell he was going to do.

What *could* he do? Through ignorance and good luck he had missed being caught when he had first tried to gain forbidden information. He couldn't try that again, not that way. The work camps in Scotland were waiting if you made trouble for the authorities. For all of his life he had looked on the camps as a stern but necessary measure to weed the troublemakers out of a highly organized society. *Prole* troublemakers of course, the thought of any other kind was unthinkable. Thinkable enough now when he might be one of them. If he did anything at all to draw attention to himself he could be caught. Just like a prole. Perhaps his sector of society was physically better off than theirs—but he was just as much a prisoner of it. What kind of a world *was* he living in? And how did he find out more about it without making that one-way trip to the Highlands?

There was no simple answer to his questions that day or the next, or the next. At the laboratory it was easy enough to get involved in his work, which was still complex and interesting. It was appreciated too.

"I cannot begin to say in words how happy I am with what you have done here," Sonia Amariglio said. "And in such a short time."

"It's been easy so far," Jan told her, spooning

sugar into his tea. It was the afternoon break and he was seriously thinking of leaving after it. "Basically what I did was upgrade the old designs. But I see where some original work will be needed very soon, particularly on the comsat twenty-one, and that will not be the easiest job."

"But you can do it. I have infinite faith! Now, to other matters. Social ones. Are you free tomorrow night?"

"I think so."

"Please be sure so. There is a reception at the Italian Embassy then and I think you will enjoy attending. The guest is someone you might enjoy meeting. Giovanni Bruno."

"Bruno? Here!"

"Yes. On the way to America for a seminar."

"I know all of his work. He's a physicist who thinks like an engineer . . ."

"I'm sure you can think of no higher praise."

"Thanks for asking me."

"A pleasure. Nine o'clock then."

Jan had no desire to attend a boring embassy party, but knew that he should not be a recluse. And if he got to talk to Bruno it might be worthwhile. The man was a genius and responsible for the whole new range of memory blocks. Probably wouldn't even be able to get near him in the press of social butterflies. He must check his evening suit to see if it needed pressing.

The crush was just what he had expected. Jan had the cab drop him a street away from the embassy and he walked the rest of the distance. All of the beautiful people were there. The ones with rank and money and no ambition other than social position. They wanted only to be seen with Bruno, to have their faces appear with his in the social columns, to talk about it afterward to acquaintances with equal interests. Jan had grown up with these people, gone to school with them, and they shared a mutual dislike one for the other. They tended to look down their noses at his family because they had a tradition of working in the sciences. There was no point in telling them that this was because of Andrzej Kulozik, a distant and revered ancestor, a physicist who had actually worked on the original and successful development of fusion power. Most of them had no idea of what fusion power was in any case. Now Jan was enveloped by them again and he did not like it. There were many familiar and half-familiar faces among the crowd in the front hall, and when he passed his coat over to the waiting porter, his own face was also fixed in the cold and distant expression he had learned in prep school.

"Jan, that is you, isn't it?" a deep voice said in his ear and he turned to see who was talking to him.

"Ricardo! A sight for sore eyes indeed."

They shook hands warmly. Ricardo de Torres, the Marquis de la Rosa, was a not too distant relation on his mother's side. Tall, elegant, black-bearded, and suave, he was about the only relative that Jan ever saw. They had been in school together and their friendship had even outlived that experience.

"Not here to meet the great man?" Ricardo asked.

"I was until I saw the receiving line for Professor Bruno. I'm not charmed in the slightest by the prospect of queuing for a half hour to press his gloved hand and hear him murmur a few words in my ear."

"How forthright your brash, island-living race has always been. I, product of an older and more leisured culture, will join the queue."

"Social obligation?"

"Right with the first guess."

"Well, while you're doing that, I am going to beat

this lionizing crowd to the buffet. I hear the kitchen here is the best."

"It is, and I envy you. For me there will be nothing but cold meats and bare bones."

"I hope not. If you live through the scrum I'll see you in there."

"Let's hope."

It was perfect; Jan had had the display of food almost to himself. A few figures wandered in front of the lengthy linen-covered table, but were far outnumbered by the servers behind it. A swarthy, white-hatted chef sharpened his knife hopefully when Jan looked at the roast; his face fell when Jan went on. He could have roast beef every day of the week. Now he was more interested in the octopus in garlic, the snails, the paté with truffles. Filling his plate with delicacies was an easy matter. The small tables against the wall were still empty and he seated himself at one to get the utmost pleasure from his food without having to juggle it on one knee. Delicious! However, a little wine was very much in order. A servant in a black dress, carrying a tray of glasses, was passing and he waved to her.

"Red. A large one," he said, his attention focused on his plate.

"Bardolino or Corvo, your honor," the waitress said.

"Corvo I believe . . . yes, Corvo."

She handed him the glass and he had to look up to take it. For the first time he saw her face. He almost dropped the glass so she took it from his hand and placed it safely on the table before him.

"*Shalom,*" Sara said, speaking very quietly. She gave him a quick wink, then turned and was gone.

Eight

Jan started to rise and go after her—then sank back into his seat. Her presence here could be no accident. And she certainly wasn't Italian. Or was she? If she were the whole story about Israel had been a hoax. For all that he knew the submarine could have been an Italian one. What was going on? His thoughts chased themselves in circles and he slowly ate the plate of delicacies without tasting one of them. By the time he had finished, the room was beginning to fill up and he knew exactly what he had to do.

Nothing too obvious; he knew the dangers of Security surveillance better than she did. His glass was empty, getting another would not be compromising. If she had come here to contact him, he wanted her to know he was aware of that. Then, if she did not get in touch with him or give him some message, her presence was an accident as far as he was concerned. Italian or Israeli she was certainly an enemy agent of some kind. In this country illegally? Did Security know about her and were they watching her even now? Should he identify her for his own protection?

He rejected the idea as soon as it was formed. He couldn't do that; whoever she was, she was also one of the people responsible for saving his life. Not only that—he had no desire to identify anyone to his brother-in-law's branch of the service. Even if he could have done it safely, for if he identified her he would have to say how he knew her and the whole story of the submarine would come out. He was beginning to realize how thin was the layer of ice that supported the world he used to call normal. He had broken through it when he had been rescued, and had been sinking deeper and deeper ever since.

It took a moment to locate her, to push through the crowd and set the empty glass on her tray. "Another Corvo, if you please." His eyes were upon her, yet she would not meet them. She passed the wine over in silence, never looking at him, turning away the instant he had taken it. So what was that supposed to mean? He was angry, feeling rejected. All of these charades just to be ignored! Or was that part of a more devious plan? The entire matter was beginning to disgust him and the noise and light was giving him a headache. Not only that but the unaccustomed spicy food sat like a weight in the pit of his stomach. There was no point in staying on here any longer.

The servant found his coat, bowing deep, holding it up so he could shrug into it. Jan went out, buttoning it, breathing deeply of the icy and refreshing air. A rank of cabs was waiting and he signaled the doorman for one. His hands were getting chilled so he pulled on one glove, then the other—and stopped.

There was something that felt like a piece of paper in the glove, at the tip of his index finger. He knew that it had not been there when he had left his apartment. For an instant he hesitated, then pulled the glove all the way on. This was neither the time nor the place to investigate. The cabby jumped out, held the door open, and saluted.

"Monument Court," he said, dropping into the seat.

The doorman hurried out from under the canopy to open the cab door when they arrived.

"Another cold one, Engineer Kulozik."

Jan nodded; there was no need to answer. He stalked across the lobby and into the elevator, not even noticing the operator who took him to his floor. Natural. He must act naturally at all times.

The alarms had not been tripped; no one had entered the apartment or tampered with anything since he had left that morning. Or if they had it had been done so well it had left no trace, in which case there was no escape. A certain fatalistic acceptance was necessary in this situation. Only when this had been done did he turn the glove inside out and shake the folded bit of paper onto the table.

It opened up to reveal a poorly printed cash register receipt for the sum of ninety-four pence. The time and date were stamped on it as well, one in the morning, some three days earlier. The establishment that had issued it was called SMITHFIELD JOLYON and he had never heard of it.

Was it an accident that this had appeared so suddenly inside his glove? No, no accident, not at the same place, the same evening he had seen Sara. It must be a message—yet a message that would be completely innocuous to anyone who might find it by accident. A register receipt; everyone had them. It would have been puzzling but meaningless to him as well if he hadn't seen her there at the embassy. So it was a message—meaning what?

The phonebook revealed that the Smithfield Jolyon was one of a chain of automated restaurants. He had never heard of them before because they were all located in areas that he never frequented. This one, while not too far away, was in a scruffy dock area. What next?

Why go there of course, at one A.M. Tonight? Of

course tonight. It would take a fool not to understand the simple intelligence carried by the slip of paper. It might also take a fool to go there. If he did not go— then what? Another attempt to contact him? Probably not. A wink was as good as a nod in this kind of business.

Jan realized that he had already made up his mind to go when he found himself considering what clothes he should wear. So it was decided. It had to be. He had to find out more. He would put on the rough clothes and boots that he used for field work in the fen district. He wouldn't look like a prole—wasn't even sure that he wanted to do that—but these clothes would be the best compromise.

At a quarter to one he parked his car in a well illuminated area of the Highway and walked the rest of the way. The streets here were not as well lit and were faced with the blank walls of warehouses. The brilliant sign of the restaurant was clearly visible ahead. It was just one o'clock. Showing no hesitancy, Jan walked slowly to the door and pushed it open.

The restaurant was not big. A large, brightly lit room with four rows of tables marching the length of it. Nor was it crowded; solitary individuals were scattered about, with one or two small groups sitting together. The air was hot and smelled strongly of antiseptic and smoke, with an underlying bite of stale food. On the rear wall was a twice-lifesize figure of a cook, constructed of garish and chipped plastic. As Jan walked slowly toward it the arm moved up and down in hesitant greeting and the computer voice spoke to him.

"Good evening . . . madam. What is your pleasure this . . . morning?"

The sex discrimination circuit did not seem to be working very well—but at least it got the time of day right. Then the chef's paunchy stomach lit up with the

71

selection of dishes; not the most appetizing location, Jan thought. He considered the selection—equally unappetizing—and finally touched the illuminated word TEA and the light went out.

"Will that be all . . . sir?" Second time around the computer got it right. He should order something else, even if he didn't eat it, in order to appear normal. He touched the glowing SAUSAGE ROLL.

"May you enjoy your repast. That will be . . . forty pence. Jolyon always happily at your service."

As soon as Jan had inserted the coins into the machine a silver dome on the wall-mounted serving trolley lifted up to display his purchases. Or at least moved halfway where it stopped, humming and vibrating. He pushed it the rest of the way and extracted the tray with cup, plate, and receipt. Only then did he turn around and look closely at the room.

Sara was not there. It took him a moment to discover this because, outside of the small groups, all of the single customers appeared to be women. Young women. And most of them were glancing his way. Quickly lowering his eyes he found the deserted end of one table and slid onto the bench mounted on the floor beside it. There were automatic dispensers fixed to the center of the table which functioned with varying degrees of success. The sugar nozzle, with much grinding, produced only a few grains; the mustard pump enthusiastically sprayed out far too much onto his sausage roll. The food was protective coloration in any case and he had no intention of eating the thing. He sipped at the tea and looked around. Sara came through the door.

He had not recognized her at first glance, not with the garish makeup and absurd coat. It was white, imitation fur, puffing out in all directions. It would not pay to watch her too closely; he put his attention back to his plate and automatically bit into the sausage roll and instantly regretted it. He quickly washed it down with some tea.

"All right if I sit here?"

She was standing across the table from him, holding her tray but not setting it down. He nodded briefly, not knowing what to say in this unusual circumstance. She took this as acceptance and set the tray with her cup of coffee down, then seated herself. Her mouth was thick with lipstick, her eyes surrounded by greenish makeup, her face expressionless under this coating. She took a sip of her coffee, then opened her coat briefly.

Under the coat she wore nothing else. He had a brief glimpse of her firm, tanned breasts before she closed it again.

"Like a good time, wouldn't you, your honor?"

So that was why the rest of the girls were here. He had heard that pickup places like this existed, schoolmates had frequented them. But this was his first encounter and he was slow with the correct response.

"Sure you'll like it," she said. "Not too expensive."

"Yes, good idea," he finally choked out. The idea of the determined woman from the submarine in this highly unusual situation almost caused him to smile. He did not, keeping his face as emotionless as hers. The ruse was a good one and not funny in the slightest. After this she said nothing else; obviously conversation in public was not one of the services being offered. When she picked up her tray and rose he stood up as well.

A light over the table began flashing on and off and a loud buzzer sounded alarmingly. Some faces turned to look in his direction.

"Pick up your tray," Sara whispered sharply.

Jan did; the light and sound stopped. He should have realized that no one would clear up after him in the automated establishment. Following her example he slid his tray into the slot beside the front door and went after her into the cold night.

"It's not too far, your honor," she said, walking quickly along the dark street. He hurried to stay by her side. Nothing else was said until she reached a grimy apartment building not far from the Thames. Sara unlocked the door, waved him through, then led the way to her rooms. When the light came on she touched her finger to her lips signaling silence, then waved him inside. Only after locking the door and examining all of the windows did she relax.

"It is good to see you again, Jan Kulozik."

"And you, Sara. A little different from the first time."

"We do seem to meet under unusual circumstances—but these are unusual times. Excuse me for a moment. I must get out of this humiliating outfit. It is the only safe way that a woman of my apparent class can meet someone of yours; the police smile on the practice. But it is still disgraceful for a woman, absolutely infuriating."

She was back in a moment wearing a warm robe. "Would you like a real cup of tea? Something better than the muck in that palace of assignation?"

"No, a drink if you have it."

"There is some Italian brandy. Stock. Very sweet but it contains alcohol."

"If you please."

She poured for both of them, then sat on the sagging couch opposite him.

"It wasn't an accident, my seeing you at the party?" he asked.

"Far from it—the entire thing was carefully orchestrated. It took a lot of money and time to set up."

"You aren't Italian, are you? I have no way of telling."

"No, I'm not. But we use them a lot when we need to. Their lower echelons are very inefficient and bribable. They are our best channel outside of our country."

"Why did you go to all this trouble to see me?"

"Because you have been thinking a lot about what you were told that day in the sub. And acting too. You almost got yourself in deep trouble. When you did that it was decided that the time had come to contact you."

"Trouble? What do you mean?"

"The business in the lab. They caught the wrong man, didn't they? It was you who was tampering with the computer files?"

Jan was afraid now. "What are you doing? Having me watched?"

"As best as we can. It's not easy. Just an informed guess that you were the one involved. That's one of the reasons it was decided to contact you now. Before you were caught doing something you shouldn't."

"Your concern across the countless miles from Israel is very touching."

Sara leaned over and took his hand in hers. "I can understand why you are angry—and I don't blame you. This entire situation has come about by accident—and it was your accident that started it."

She sat back and sipped her drink and, for some reason, the brief human contact calmed him.

"When we saw your yacht sunk and the two of you in the water there was some furious debate as to what we should do. When the original plan failed we jury-rigged a second one to compromise you. Giving you enough information so that if you revealed any of it you would be in as much trouble as we would be."

"Then it was no accident that you talked to me as you did?"

"No. I'm sorry if you think we took advantage of

you, but it was our own survival as well. I'm a security officer so it was my job to do it . . ."

"Security! Like Thurgood-Smythe?"

"Not quite like your brother-in-law. The opposite if anything. But let me bring you up to date first. We saved you and the girl because you were people in need. That was all. But once saved, we had to keep track of you to see what you would say about the matter. Thank you for doing what you did. It is greatly appreciated."

"So well appreciated that you have been keeping tabs on me ever since?"

"This is a completely different matter. We saved your life, you did not reveal our existence. The two acts cancel out, that matter is over with."

"It will never be over with. That little seed of doubt you planted has been growing well ever since."

Sara shrugged with both hands held wide. An ancient gesture that conveyed resignation, the hand of fate—yet contained also an element of what-is-done-is-done.

"Have some more to drink. At least it is warming," she said, reaching over with the bottle. "While watching you we discovered who you were, what you did. There was enthusiasm in high places. If you had returned to your normal life you would never have heard from us again. But you did not. So I am here this evening."

"Welcome to London. What do you want from me?"

"Your help, technical help that is."

"What do you offer in return?"

"Why the entire world. Nothing less." Her smile was wide and happy, her teeth smooth and white. "We will be pleased to tell you the true history of the world, what really happened in the past and is happening in the present. What lies are being told and

76

what unrest is developing. It makes a fascinating story. Do you want to hear it?"

"I'm not sure. What will happen to me if I do get involved?"

"You will be an important part of an international conspiracy that is hoping to overthrow the ruling governments of the world and restore democracy to those who have been deprived of it for centuries."

"Is that all?"

They both laughed at that and some of the tension went out of the air. "You had better think carefully before you answer," Sara said. "There are very great dangers involved."

"I think I made the decision the moment I lied to Security. I'm in too deep now and I know so little. I must know it all."

"And so you shall. Tonight." She went to the window, opened the curtains, and looked out. Then closed them again and sat down.

"John will be here in a few minutes and will answer all your questions. This meeting was difficult to set up so it was agreed to make the most of it if you went along. I've just let them know that. John is not his real name of course. And you will be called Bill for the same reason. And he will be wearing one of these. Just slip it over your head."

She passed over a soft, masklike object.

"What is it?"

"Face changer. It has built in thickenings and pressure plates. Your chin will be wider, nose flatter, cheeks hollower, that kind of thing. And dark glasses will hide your eyes. Then, if the worst happens, you can't identify John—he can't accuse you."

"But you know me. What if you are caught?"

Before Sara could answer there was a rapid bleeping from the turned-off radio. Four quick notes and no more. The effect was remarkable.

She was on her feet in an instant, tearing the face-changer from his hand and running swiftly into the other room. "Take your jacket off, open your shirt," she called back over her shoulder. She returned in a few moments wearing a very transparent black gown trimmed with pink lace. There was a knock on the door.

"Who is it?" she asked, calling through the thin paneling.

"Police," was the short, shocking answer.

Nine

When the door was opened the uniformed officer ignored Sara, just pushing past her and crossing to Jan who was still sitting in the chair, glass in hand. The policeman had a riot helmet on with its transparent faceplate lowered. His uniform was thick, padded with layers of woven armor, while his fingers stayed close to the large automatic that swung arrogantly from his hip. He stopped in front of Jan and looked him up and down slowly.

Jan took a sip from the glass and was determined to show no guilt, no matter how bad the situation was.

"What are you doing here?" Jan snapped.

"Sorry, your honor. Routine." The policeman's words were muffled by the faceplate and he swung it open. His expression was blank, professional. "We've had some gentlemen molested by the tarts, sir, and their fancy men. Can't have that in a law-abiding city. Straightened up now, but this one is a new one. Foreigner. Italian, just over here for a while on a temporary. Don't mind her making a bit of extra crumble on the side, novelty for the gentlemen you might say, but we also don't want any trouble. Everything all right, sir?"

"Quite all right—until you came barging in."

"I can understand your feelings, sir. But it is illegal, don't you forget, your honor." There was steel-beneath the calm words; Jan knew better than to force the issue. "Just looking after your best interests. Have you been in the other rooms yet?"

"No."

"Then I'll just have a look-round. Never know what you find under these beds sometimes."

Jan and Sara looked at each other in silence while the policeman stamped heavily through the rooms and finally returned.

"All in order, your honor. Enjoy yourself. Good night."

He let himself out and Jan found himself shaking with rage, flushed and angry. He raised his fist to the closed door as Sara grabbed him around the shoulders and pressed her finger to his lips.

"They do that all the time, your honor. Bust in, boom, looking for trouble. They lie, all of them. Now we have a nice time and you forget."

She held him tightly while she talked and his anger waned as he became aware of the warmth and closeness of her firm body through the thin material of her gown.

"Have another of this good Italian drink," she said, pulling away and crossing to the table. She rattled her glass against the bottle with her left hand while she quickly scribbled a note on a pad with her right. When she came back it was the note she gave him, not the drink.

MAYBE RECORDER OTHER ROOM. YOU ANGRY. LEAVE NOW.

"I'm not sure I want another drink. Do you usually have the police bursting through your door at all hours?"

"It means nothing . . ."

"It means a lot to me. Get my coat. I'm getting out of here."

"But money. You promised."

"Two pounds for the drinks is all you'll get."

When she handed him the coat she had another note ready. YOU'LL BE CONTACTED it read. She squeezed his hand in hers—then kissed him swiftly on the cheek before she let him out.

Almost a week passed before Jan was contacted again. His work in the lab improved when he found that he could now devote his entire attention to it. Though he was still in danger, probably more danger than before since he was consorting with the underground, he was more relaxed. Less lonely. That was the important thing. Until he had talked with Sara, brief as the meeting had been, there had been no one to confide in, no one to talk with about the momentous discoveries and doubts. That solitary existence had ended, would be ended, since he had no doubt that contact would be reestablished soon.

It had been his habit for some weeks now to go into a bar close to the satellite laboratories for a drink or two before going home. The barman, fat, friendly, was a specialist in mixed drinks and devilish concoctions. There seemed to be no end to his repertoire and Jan had settled on a half dozen of the more interesting ones.

"Brian, what was the name of that bittersweet thing I had here a few days ago?"

"A negroni cocktail, your honor, speciality of Italy. Would you like one?"

"Yes. It appears to have great relaxing powers."

Jan was sipping at it, his mind still on orientation circuits for solar cell banks, when someone sat on the stool next to him. Female he was aware of that when the rich mink coat brushed his arm. The voice was very familiar though the accent wasn't.

"Why Jan! It is Jan Kulozik, isn't it?"

It was Sara, but a very different Sara. Her makeup and clothes were in the same class as her coat—as was her accent. "Why, hello," was the best he could come up with.

"I was sure it was you, though I bet you don't remember little me, Cynthia Barton, we met at that dreadful party a few weeks ago. Whatever you're drinking looks divine; order me up one like a good lad."

"Nice to see you again."

"Nicer to see you, it's been one of those days. Hmmm, this is simply super, just what the doctor ordered. But don't you find it hideously noisy in here, the music and all these people? Let's drink these and go back to your place. I remember you were very insistent about a painting there you wanted me to see. At the time I thought it was just an excuse to get into my knickers, but now I don't know. You're such a serious chap that perhaps you *do* have a painting and I'll risk my honor to find out."

There was more like this, even in the cab, and Jan found that he need not answer but just let himself be washed along on the tide of words. Only after his apartment door was closed did she stop talking and look to him for a lead.

"It's all right," he said. "I've installed a number of alarms, bug detectors and the telltale, that lamp bulb, says all clear. If it were out I would know there had been some tampering. Dare I ask who Cynthia Barton is?"

Sara threw her coat on the chair and looked around the room. "Someone who looks a good deal like me. Not a duplicate by any means, but the same general size and hair color. When she's away—she's at a country house in Yorkshire this week—I use her persona to move in better circles. My ID is pretty good, enough for any casual identification."

"I'm glad she's away. It's nice to see you again."

"The feeling is mutual because there have been some rapid developments since I talked to you last."

"Like what?"

"I'll tell you in a little while, in context. I want you to get a clearer picture of the entire situation first. The man you were supposed to meet last time, code name John, is on his way over here now. I came first to let you know what was happening. You've got a stunning place here," she added, with rapid change of subject.

"I can't take any credit. When I bought it I was going out with a girl who had pretences of being an interior decorator. With my money and her talent this is what we got."

"Why do you say 'pretences'? She seems quite good."

"Well, you know, it's not really a woman's field."

"Male chauvinist pig."

"What does that mean? It doesn't sound nice."

"It isn't. An archaic term of contempt—and I apologize. It's not your fault. You have been raised in a strictly male-oriented society where women are respected, but still second-class citizens . . ." A chime rang and she raised her eyebrows in query.

"That's the entrance. Could it be John?"

"It should be. He was given a key to the garage entrance of this building and told to come to this apartment number. As far as he knows it is just a safe house where we are meeting; he has no way of discovering that you live here. It's not perfect, I know, but it's the best we could do in a hurry. In any case he is not an active man in the organization and there is little contact with him, other than as an information source. Better put this on." Sara took a face-changer from her purse. "And the dark glasses too. I'll let him in."

In the bathroom Jan pulled the flexible disguise over his head and the effect was astonishing. When he looked into the mirror a stranger stared back. If he didn't recognize himself then he would never be able to identify the man called John. If he wore one of these as well.

Sara was talking to a short, stocky man when he returned. Though he had taken off his overcoat he was still wearing his hat and gloves. Hair and hands invisible. Sara was undisguised which meant that her identity was known to them both. "John," she said. "This is Bill. The man who wants to ask you some questions."

"Happy to be of service, Bill." His voice was mellow, educated. "What do you want to know?"

"I don't know where to begin, what to ask. I know some things about Israel that differ from texts I have—and I suppose that is the extent of my knowledge. Other than what I was taught in school."

"Well that's a good beginning. You have doubts and you have seen that the world is not as you always suspected. So I shan't waste time trying to convince you to open your mind. May we sit down?"

John settled into his chair and crossed his legs comfortably. When he talked he tended to lecture, to tick off the points made on his fingers. It was obvious he was an academic of some kind, probably an historian.

"Let us go back to the close of the twentieth century and look closely at events since that date. Let your mind be a *tabula rasa* and try not to interrupt with questions. There'll be time enough later for those. The world of the year 2000 was very much as depicted in the historical texts you have studied, physically that is, although the governments of the world were definitely *not* what you have been told. At that time there were varying degrees of personal freedom throughout the world, with forms of government ranging from the liberal to the most oppressive. All of that has changed in the intervening years. The Wreckers were to blame for it all, just as you have learned. That much at least is true." He coughed. "My dear, might I have a glass of water?"

Sara brought it to him and he went on.

"None of the world leaders or governments, the Wreckers, took any real notice of the depletion of natural resources until it was too late. Populations expanded past the limit of natural resources, while the supplies of fossil fuels quickly ran out. There was much fear of an atomic war that would devastate the world, but apparently the fear was mutually felt among the world powers because the big bang never came. Of course there were some atomic incidents in Africa, using what were quaintly referred to as homemade atomic bombs, but these petered out quickly enough. The world did not end with the bang, as had been feared, but with a whimper. I quote the poet."

He sipped daintily from his glass and went on.

"With no energy, factory after factory closed. With no fuel vehicles could not run and the economies of the world spiraled downward into depression and massive unemployment. The weaker and more unstable nations went by the board, torn apart by starvation and dissent. The stronger nations had enough worries at home without attempting to cope with the troubles of others. The surviving citizens of what used to be called the third world eventually stabilized with small populations and basic agrarian economies.

"A different solution was needed for the developed, industrial economies. I will use Britain to demonstrate this, since you are familiar with what life here has become. You must cast your mind back to an earlier day when the form of government was democratic, regular elections were held, and the Houses of

Parliament were not hereditary and powerless as they are now. Democracy, where all individuals are held to be equal, one man one vote to elect the rulers, is a luxury of the very rich. By that I mean very rich countries. Any decline in living standards and the national product can only mean a lessening of democracy. A simple example. An employed man with a regular income has a choice of dwelling, diet, recreation, what might be called lifestyle. An unemployed man on the dole must live where he is told, eat what he is given, and accommodate himself to an unchanging and unvarying, drab existence. Britain survived the disaster years—but paid a terrible price in personal freedom. There was no money to import food, so the country had to be self-sufficient agriculturally. This meant microscopic amounts of meat, only for the very rich, and a vegetarian diet for the rest. A meat-eating nation does not easily take to a change like this so the change had to be enforced. The ruling elite issued the orders and police and troops saw that they were carried out. This was the only alternative to chaos, famine, and death at the time, so it seemed reasonable. And it *was* reasonable given the circumstances. The only trouble was that when the emergency lifted and things were physically much better, the ruling elite liked the authority they had and did not want to relinquish it. A great thinker once wrote that power corrupts and absolute power corrupts absolutely. Once the hobnailed boot is firmly planted on the neck it will not be raised voluntarily."

"What hobnailed boot?" Jan asked, puzzled.

"I do beg your pardon. A simile, very out of date, excuse the excess. I mean to say that recovery was gradual and the governments in power simply stayed in power. Populations gradually reduced and stabilized at a replacement level. The first generating satellites were built and beamed their energy down to

Earth. Then came fusion power that assured abundant energy for all needs. Mutated plants supplied the chemicals formerly obtained from petroleum. Satellite colonies processed the raw materials of the moon and their manufactured products were brought to Earth. The discovery of a workable space drive sent ships out to explore and settle on the planets of the nearest stars. So there we have it, what we have today. An earthly paradise, even a heavenly paradise, where no man need fear war or famine. Where all are provided for and none need want.

"However there is one thing wrong with this picture of paradise. Absolute oligarchic rule has clamped down on the countries of Earth, extended to the satellite colonies, and beyond them to the planets. The rulers of each major country are in collusion with all of the other rulers to assure that no hint of personal freedom be allowed the masses. Complete freedom at the top—your class, Bill, from your accent—and economic serfdom, slavery, for all below. With instant imprisonment or death for any bold enough to protest."

"Is it really that bad?" Jan asked.

"It's far worse than you can imagine," Sara said. "And you will have to see for yourself. Until you are absolutely convinced that there is need for a change you will be a danger to yourself and others."

"This orientation program has been carried out at my suggestion," John said, unable to keep the pedantic pride from his voice. "It is one thing to read printed documents and hear spoken words. It is another to experience the realities of the world we live in. Only a brute would be unmoved. I will talk to you again after your descent into the inferno. I will let myself out, if I may."

"He's a funny little man," Jan said after the outside door had closed.

"Funny and endearing and absolutely invaluable

87

to us. A social theoretician with answers rather than questions."

Jan pulled off the face-changer and wiped the perspiration from his face. "Obviously an academic, probably an historian . . ."

"Don't!" Sara said sharply. "Don't theorize about him, even to yourself, or one day you may reveal him to those who shouldn't know. Put the man from your thoughts and remember his words. Can you take off a few days from your work?"

"Any time, of course. I make my own hours. What do you want?"

"Tell them that you need a break and you want to go to the country, to see a friend, something like that, where it won't be too easy to trace you."

"What about skiing? I usually go to Scotland once or twice a winter for cross country."

"I don't know what that is."

"Special kind of skis for going on the flat, not downhill. I carry a pack, camp out a bit, stay in inns and hotels, make my own way."

"That sounds ideally perfect. So tell your people that you are going skiing, starting next Tuesday, for a few days. Don't be specific about how long you will be away. Don't mention any addresses or places in particular. Pack a bag and put it in your car."

"Will I be going to Scotland?"

"No. You will be going even farther away. You are going to descend into that inferno right here in London."

Ten

Jan had been parked at the appointed spot for over a half an hour, well past the time when he was to have been met. Outside only the yellow gleams of the streetlights could be seen through the swirling snow. The pavements were empty. The dark bulk of Primrose Hill vanished into the darkness beyond the road. The only traffic had been a police car that had driven by earlier, slowed a bit, then speeded up and vanished. Perhaps he was being watched for some reason and his contact would not appear.

Even as he thought this the door opened letting in a blast of frigid air. A heavily bundled man slid into the passenger seat, closing the door quickly behind him.

"You wouldn't like to say something, would you, gov?" the man said.

"It's going to get a lot colder before it gets warmer."

"You're right about that." Sara had briefed him with the identification phrase. "What else do you know?"

"Nothing. I was told to park here, wait for someone, identify myself, and wait for instructions."

"Right. Or it's going to be right if you take the instructions and do everything exactly like I say to do

89

it. You're what you are and I'm a prole and you are going to have to take your orders from me. Can you?"

"I don't see why not." Jan inwardly cursed the hesitancy in his voice. This wasn't easy.

"Do you really mean it? Obey a prole—and one that don't smell too good?"

Now that he had mentioned it there was a definite stench in the air from his heavy clothes. Long unwashed fabric and body odor mixed with traces of smoke and cooking.

"I mean it," Jan said, in sudden anger. "I don't think it is going to be easy but I'll do my best. And I'll live with the smell too."

There was a silence and Jan could see the man's eyes, barely visible under his cloth cap, examining him closely. He suddenly shot out a gnarled hand.

"Put it there, gov. I think you're going to be all right." Jan found his hand clamped in a calloused, hard grip. "I was told to call you John, and John it is. I'm called Fryer since I work in a chipper, so we'll leave it at that. If you'll just head east now I'll call out turnings."

There was very little traffic about and the tires cut black marks in the freshly fallen snow. They stayed off the main roads and Jan had very little idea of where they were exactly, just northeast London.

"Almost there," Fryer said. "Another mile to go, but we can't drive. Slow now, it's the second turning on the left."

"Why can't we drive?"

"Security barrier. Nothing to be seen of course, you wouldn't know you were going past it. But circuitry under the road surface would query the transponder in your car and get its identity. Goes in the record. Start people wondering what you're doing here. Walking over is safer, though a lot colder."

"I never knew they did anything like that."

"This is going to be an educational holiday for you, John. Slow—stop. I'll open that lockup garage and you just edge this vehicle in. It'll be safe enough here."

The garage was cold and musty. Jan waited in the darkness while Fryer closed and locked the door, then shuffled by, finding his way with the light from a small flashlight. There was a room beyond, a shed behind the garage, lit by a single unshielded light bulb. Fryer turned on a single-bar electric fire which did little or nothing to relieve the chill of the room.

"Here's where we make the change, gov," Fryer said, taking some rough clothes down from a peg on the wall. "I see you didn't shave today as told, very wise. And your boots will do, after we scuff them up a bit and rub in some ashes. But off with the rest, from the small clothes out."

Jan tried not to shiver, but it proved impossible to control. The thick, stained trousers were like ice on his already cold legs. Rough shirt, waistcoat with buttons missing, ragged sweater, even more ragged greatcoat. However once the chill was off of everything it proved warm enough.

"Didn't know your hat size so I got this," Fryer said, holding up a hand-knitted balaclava. "Best thing for this weather anyway. Sorry to say it, but you'll have to leave behind those fine fur gloves. Not many on the dole have gloves. Just jam your hands into your pockets and you'll be all right. That's it, wonderful. Your own mam would never recognize you in the rig. So here we go."

Once they were moving through the dark streets it was not too bad. The wool of the balaclava covered Jan's mouth and nose, his hands were buried in the deep pockets, his feet warm enough in the old climbing boots he had unearthed in the back of his closet. His mood was good for there was a spirit of adventure in this whole affair.

"You better keep your mouth shut unless I tell you it's OK, gov. One word from you and they'll all know who you are. Time now for a half liter, thirsty work this. Just drink what you're given and say naught."

"What if someone talks to me?"

"They won't. It's not that kind of pub."

A blast of warm, noisome air blew over them when they pushed through the heavy front door. Men, only men, sitting at tables and standing at the bar. Some were eating plates of food served through a hatch in one wall. Stew of some kind, Jan saw when they squeezed past a crowded table, along with chunks of dark bread. There was room at the scarred, damp bar and they stood there while Fryer signaled one of the barmen.

"Two halfs of skrumpy," he said, then confided in Jan, "mild's like swill here, better the cider."

Jan grunted assent and buried his face in the glass when it came. Acid and terrible. What could the beer possibly be like!

Fryer was right; this was not a sociable bar. Men were talking together who had obviously arrived together. Those who were alone stayed alone, seeking communion only with their drink. An air of depression hung over the dark room unchallenged by the stained brewery posters on the walls, the only decoration of any kind. The drinkers were obviously seeking oblivion not relaxation. Jan drank deep when Fryer moved away in the crowd. He returned in a moment with another man, appearing no different from the others in his rumpled dark clothes.

"We'll go now," Fryer said, making no attempt to introduce the man. Once outside they tramped through the snow, now beginning to drift over the curbs, their footsteps silent in its softness.

"My mate here knows a lot of people," Fryer said,

nodding his head in the direction of their new acquaintance. "Knows everyone. Knows everything going on here in Islington."

"Been inside too," the man said, his words very liquid and lisping. He appeared to have very few teeth in his head. "Caught using the stuff. Hard work cutting them trees in Scotland. Cured the habit though. The hard way. This old woman now, you'll see how she lives. Not much of a life but she'll be well out of it soon."

They turned in through the gates of a brooding rank of tall council flats, crossing the open area between them. It could have been grassed or paved, impossible to tell now. Spotlights high up on the building lit the area like a prison yard, spilling brightly over the children who were building a giant snowman. An altercation broke out and they fell to shouting and beating one small boy who finally broke from them and ran away crying loudly, leaving a trail of red drops in the snow behind him. Neither of Jan's companions seemed aware of the scene so Jan put it from his mind as well.

"Lifts not working. Usual thing," Fryer said as they followed their guide up the steps. Up five filthy flights, the walls daubed all the way with graffiti. Warm enough though, as it should be with unlimited electric power. The door was locked but the man had a key. They followed him into a single warm, brightly lit room that smelled of death.

"She don't look good, do she?" he said, gesturing toward the woman on the bed.

She was pale as parchment, her skin lighter than the stained covers of the bed. One clawlike hand held them clutched under her chin and her unconscious breathing was slow, scratchy.

"You can talk if you want," Fryer said. "All friends here."

"She's ill?" Jan said.

"Ill to death your honor," the toothless man said. "Saw doctor in the autumn, got some medicine, nothing since."

"She should be in hospital."

"Hospital only for dying on the dole."

"A doctor then."

"Can't go to him. Won't come here without no money."

"But there must be funds available from . . . our people."

"There are," Fryer said. "More than enough to at least help our mates. We don't dare, gov. Go on her record, the Security will want to know where did she get the crumble on the dole, investigation, find out who her friends are. Do more harm than good. So we don't do it."

"So—she just dies?"

"We all die sooner or later. Just sooner on the dole. Let's go get some scoff."

They did not say good-bye to the toothless man who had drawn up a chair and was sitting next to the bed. Jan looked at the box of a room, the decrepit furniture, the sanitary fittings on the wall, barely concealed by a battered screen. A prison cell would be better.

"He'll be with us after a bit," Fryer said. "Wants to sit awhile with his mam."

"The woman—his mother?"

"Indeed. Happens to all of us."

They descended to the basement, to a communal dining room. The dole obviously did not extend to the luxury of private cooking. People of all ages were sitting at the rough tables, eating, or queuing at the steaming counter.

"Put this in the slot when you take your tray," Fryer said, handing Jan a red plastic token.

94

The tray did not come free in his hand until the token dropped. Jan shuffled behind Fryer, accepting the brimming bowl thrust at him by the perspiring kitchen assistant. Further on there was a great mound of chunks of dark bread and he took one. This was dinner. They seated themselves at a table bare of any condiments or tableware.

"How do I eat it?" Jan asked, looking dubiously at his bowl.

"With a spoon you always carries—but I've an extra knowing you're new at this."

It was a lentil stew with vegetable bits floating in it. Not bad tasting, devoid of any real flavor of anything. There were lumps in it that looked like meat, but certainly didn't taste like it.

"Got some salt in my pocket if you want," Fryer volunteered.

"No thanks. I doubt if it would make any difference." He ate some bread which, though half stale, had a sound, nutty flavor. "No meat in the meal?"

"No. Not ever on the dole. There's chunks of soy immo here, all the protein you need they say. Water at the fountain over there if you want to wash it down."

"Afterward. Is the food always like this?"

"More or less. People earn a bit of money they buy bits of things in the shops. If you've no crumble then this is it. You can live on it."

"I suppose that you could. But I don't really see it as an inspiring regular diet." He shut up as a man came in, shambled over, and sat at their table.

"Bit of trouble, Fryer," he said, looking at Jan while he did.

They stood and moved against the wall to talk. Jan ate another spoonful then pushed the bowl away from him. A lifetime eating this? Nine out of ten workers were on the dole. Not to mention their wives and children. And this had been going on around him for all of his life—and he had not been aware. He had lived his life on an iceberg, unaware of the buried nine-tenths beneath the surface.

"We're going back to the car, gov," Fryer said. "Something's come up."

"Anything to do with me?"

"Don't know. Word just passed for us to get there as soon as we could. No idea of what, except it's trouble. Plenty of it."

They walked hard. Not running, that would draw attention, but solidly and steadily through the clutching snow. Jan had glimpses of lit shops with their displays hidden behind steamy windows. He wondered what they sold, and realized they were as alien to his experience as the shops in the market he had visited on the shore of the Red Sea.

At the rear of the garage once again, Jan held the flashlight so that Fryer could find the right key in its dim light. They went into the shed and on into the garage itself.

"I'll be winged!" Fryer said, flashing the light across the barren floor.

"My car is gone!"

A far brighter torch flashed in their eyes and someone said, "Just stand right there and don't move. Watch where you put your hands."

Eleven

Jan had no thought of moving, could not have moved if he had wanted to. The shock of all this, first his car gone, then the sudden confrontation. The game was up, he was caught, it was all over. He stood, frozen with the dreadful realization.

"Back to the shed, Fryer," the man said again. "Someone here you don't know."

Fryer went out docilely enough and the man with the flashlight followed him; Jan could only make out his outline as he went by. What was happening?

"Jan, I must talk to you," a familiar voice said as soon as the door had closed. The small light was still in his hand and he brought it up and picked Sara's face out of the darkness. "We didn't mean to give you a fright," she said, "but this is an emergency."

"Fright! It was nothing like that. My heart stopped, that was all!"

"I'm sorry," she smiled, but the smile instantly vanished. "Something very bad has happened and we may need your help. One of our people has been captured and we cannot let him be identified. Have you heard of Slethill Camp?"

"No."

"It's a work camp in Sunderland, the far north of Scotland in the Highlands. We are fairly sure that we can get him out of the camp, that is easy enough, but we don't know how to get him out of the area. That is when I thought of you and your saying you go up there for cross-country skiing. Could he ski out of there?"

"He could if he knew the area and knew how to ski. Does he?"

"No, I don't think so. But he's young and fit and could learn. Is it difficult?"

"Very easy to learn the basics. Very hard to be very good. Do you have anyone who could show him what to do . . ." Sudden realization struck him and he turned the light back on her face. Her eyes were lowered and she was very pale.

"Yes. I'm going to ask you to help," Sara said. "It bothers me not only for the danger you will be put in, but because we should not even be mentioning this sort of thing to you. If you decide to work with us, yours could be the most important job in the entire resistance. But if this man is not freed it might very well be the end of everything."

"It's that important?"

"It is."

"Then of course I'll help. But I must go home for my equipment—"

"Impossible. Everyone thinks that you are in Scotland. We have even had your car driven up there to cover your movements here."

"So that's where it went."

"We can have it left wherever you want in Scotland. Will that help?"

"Tremendously. How do I get there?"

"By train. There's one leaving for Edinburgh in two hours and we can get you on it. You'll go as you are, you won't be noticed that way, and you can bring your other clothes in a bag. Fryer will go with you."

Jan thought swiftly, frowning into the darkness.

"Arrange it then. Also arrange to meet me yourself in Edinburgh in the morning, in your Cynthia Barton role, and bring some money. At least five hundred pounds in cash. Old notes. Can that be done?"

"Of course. I'll take care of it now. Fryer will be informed of everything. Call to him now, tell him the man with him is to leave with me."

It seemed foolish, that people risking their lives together could not even see each other's faces. But it was simple insurance that if one of them were captured he could not identify the others. They stayed in darkness until Fryer and the unknown man returned, then he and Sara left in silence after a quick muttered conversation with Fryer. Fryer waited until they left before he turned the light on.

"Going for a mystery tour are we," he said. "Nice time of year for a trip." He rooted in the boxes at the end of the garage and produced an ancient army duffle bag. "This will do fine. Just put your clothes in here and we'll be off. A brisk walk should get us to King's Cross just on time."

Once more Fryer showed his superior knowledge of the back streets of London. Only twice were they forced to cross any of the brilliantly lit avenues. Each time Fryer scouted ahead first to make sure they would not be observed, before he led Jan to the security of the darkness on the other side. They reached King's Cross station with forty-five minutes to spare. The funny thing was that Jan, who had been here countless times before on the way to Scotland, did not recognize it.

They turned off the street into a long tunnel. Despite the fact that it was well illuminated it still had been used as a latrine and the smell of urine was sharp in the air. Their footsteps echoed as they went through it and up the stairs at the other end, into a large waiting room filled with scuffed benches. Most

of the occupants seemed to be stretched out and
sound asleep, although there were a few sitting up,
waiting for their trains. Fryer went to the battered
cigarette machine and dug a metal box from his
pocket which he put under the dispenser. When the
machine was satisfied that he had inserted enough
small change, it rattled briefly and disgorged some
cigarettes into the box. He handed it to Jan, along
with a glow lighter.

"Here. Smoke a bit. Try to look natural. Don't
talk to anyone no matter what they say. I'll get the
tickets."

The cigarettes were a brand Jan had never heard
of before; WOODBINE was printed in blue letters the
length of each of them, and they crackled like smoldering straw when lit, and burned his mouth.

There was a slow movement of people in and out
of the waiting room, but no one as much as bothered
to glance his way. Every few minutes the tannoy
speakers would garble out an incomprehensible an-
nouncement. Jan grubbed his third cigarette out, feeling slightly bilious, when Fryer came back.

"Right as rain, gov. Off to the land of the Scots,
but let's go to the bog first. Do you have a bandana
with you?"

"In my pocket, here in the bag."

"Well dig it out now, we're going to need it. People sit close in these trains, nosy parkers, talk like old
women. And we don't want you doing any talking."

In the washroom Jan recoiled as Fryer snicked
out an immense blade from his pocket knife. "Minor
surgery, gov, for your own good. Keep you alive it
will. Now if you'll just peel your lip back I'm going to
make a little nick in your gum. You won't feel a thing."

"It hurts like hell," Jan said thickly through the
white kerchief he pressed to his mouth. He took it
away and saw it stained with blood.

"That's the way. Good and red. If it starts to heal up just open it again with your tongue. And spit a bit of blood once in a while. Be convincing. Now here we go. I'll bring the bag, you keep that kerchief in front of your mouth."

There was a separate entrance to the Flying Scotsman platform that Jan had never known existed, admitting them to the rear of the train. Far ahead Jan could see the lights and scurrying porters at the first-class section behind the engine, where he always traveled. A private compartment, a drink from the recessed bar if he wanted it, then a good night's sleep to wake up in Glasgow. He knew that there was a second-class section because he had seen them boarding, crowding into their multitiered sleeping coaches, waiting patiently in the station in Scotland until the first-class passengers had disembarked. He had never even suspected that there was a third-class section.

The coaches were warm, that was all that could be said for them; there was no bar, no buffet, no services of any kind. The seats were built of wood lathes, constructed for durability only and not for style or comfort. Jan managed to find a window seat so he could lean back in the corner, resting his head on his bundle of clothing. Fryer sat down solidly next to him, lighting a cigarette and blowing the smoke complacently in the direction of the NO SMOKING sign. Others crowded in and were still seating themselves when the train slid gently into motion.

It was a very uncomfortable journey. Jan's handkerchief was well speckled with blood and he had even managed one carmined expectoration following his companion's orders. After that he tried to sleep, difficult under the bright lights that remained on all night. Despite Fryer's fears no one talked to them, or even noticed him after a first interested examination of his bloodstained mouth. The train rumbled on and he did finally fall asleep, waking up with a start at the firm shake on his shoulder.

"Rise and shine, old son," Fryer said. "Half six of a lovely morning and you can't spend the whole day in bed. Let's get some breakfast."

Jan's mouth tasted terrible and he was sore and stiff from sitting on the slatted bench all night. But the long walk down the platform in the cold air woke him up and the sight of the steamed windows of the buffet made him realize that he was hungry, very hungry indeed. Breakfast was simple, but enjoyable and filling. Fryer paid out the coins for their tea and brimming bowls of porridge and Jan wolfed his down. A man, dressed as they were, put a cup of tea on the table and sat down next to Fryer.

"Eat up, lads, and come wi' me. There's no' much time."

They took the lift out of the station and followed him in silence as he walked briskly through the cold of the dawn fog, into an apartment building not too distant from the station, up endless flights of stairs—were the lifts always in need of repair?—and into a grimy flat that, except for having more rooms, could have been a duplicate of the one they had visited in London. Jan stood at the sink and shaved with an ancient razor, trying not to nick himself too badly, then put his own clothes back on. With a feeling of relief, he had to admit. He tried not to consider the thought that if he had been that uncomfortable in these clothes, in these surroundings, for less than a day—how would a lifetime of it feel? He was tired; it didn't bear considering now. The other two men watched with solid indifference. Fryer held up the boots that he had been working on with dark polish.

"Not too bad, gov. You wouldn't want to go to no dances in them, but they'll do for the street. And I have a message that a certain person will be waiting for you in the lobby of the Caledonian Hotel. If you'll follow our friend here he'll lead you right to it."

"And you?"

"Never ask questions, gov. But I'm for home as soon as I can. Too cold up here in the north." His smile showed a number of blackened teeth; he took Jan's hand. "Good luck."

Jan followed his guide into the street and stayed a good twenty meters behind him as they walked. The sun had burned away the fog and the cold air felt good. As they passed the Caledonian Hotel the man shrugged his shoulder, then hurried on. Jan pushed through the revolving door and saw Sara sitting under a potted palm reading a newspaper. Or appearing to, for before he could walk over she stood and crossed in front of him, apparently without noticing him, and exited through the side entrance. He went after her and found her waiting for him around the corner.

"It's all been arranged," she said. "Everything ex-cept the skis. You will be boarding a train at eleven this morning."

"That will be enough time for our shopping. You have the money?" She nodded "Good, then here is what we will do. I have been thinking about it most of the night—plenty of opportunity for that where I was. Were you on the train too?"

"Yes, in second class. It was bearable."

"All right. We have three shops to go to, the only three sporting goods places in Edinburgh that sell ski equipment. We'll make the purchases between us, us-ing cash so there will be no record of credit card use. They know me here, and I'll say I lost my card on the train and it will be an hour before a new one can be issued, in the meantime I want to buy a few things. I know it works this way because it happened to me a few years ago. They'll take the cash."

"It will work for one, but not for two. I have a

103

card for an account that is solvent, though the person named on the card does not exist."

"That's even better. You'll buy the expensive items like the high density battery and two compasses I'll need. Do you want me to write down what you should get?"

"No. I have been trained to remember things."

"Good. You mentioned a train. What will I be doing then?"

"Both of us will be going to Inverness for the night. You are well known at Kingsmills Hotel, aren't you?"

"You people know more about me than I do myself. Yes, they know me there."

"We thought so. A room has been booked for you for the night. By morning everything else will have been arranged."

"You can't tell me yet what is being planned?"

"I don't know myself. This whole thing has been rush and extemporize and pulled together at the last minute. But we do have a solid base in the Highlands, ex-prisoners for the most part who are glad to help escapers. They know by experience what it is like inside."

They stepped into a doorway so she could give him the money. He told her what would be needed and she nodded her head and repeated the list word-perfect.

When they met again he had his purchases in a backpack, but the skis and everything else she had bought had been sent ahead to the station, to be put into his compartment. They reached the station a half an hour before the train was to leave and Jan made a detailed search of the compartment, as detailed as he could without instruments, for any concealed bugs.

"Nothing that I can find," he said.

"To our knowledge these compartments are rarely

bugged, unless for a specific assignment. It is different in second class where bugging and computer monitoring are routine."

Sara had taken off her coat and sat by the window as the train started, looking out as the buildings gave way to countryside. Her green suit appeared to be soft leather, trimmed with fur that matched her fur hat. She turned and caught his eyes on her.

"I was admiring," he said. "You look very attractive in that getup."

"Protective coloration, a beautiful woman of means. But thank you in any case. Though I believe in complete equality of the sexes it does not offend me, as it does some, to be admired for something other than my brain."

"How could it offend?" Jan was still stopped by some of the things she said. "But don't tell me—not just now. I'm going to open the bar and give you a drink of something strong, and myself one as well, then ring for some sandwiches with meat in them." He felt a flash of guilt which he tried to ignore. "Venison, they do it very well on this train. And perhaps some smoked salmon first. And with it—yes, here it is—Glen Morangie, the finest of the straight malt whiskies. Do you know it?"

"I have never even heard of it."

"Lucky girl, to roll in warm luxury through the cold Highland wilderness—sipping your first malt. I'll join you."

It was impossible not to enjoy the trip, despite the danger it represented. This danger was in the past—and the future. For the brief hours they were on the train the world was held in suspension. Outside the window the sun shone brilliantly on a white landscape of mountains and forest, the occasional flatness of a frozen loch. No smoke rose from the chimneys of the crofters' cottages, even the most remote of them was heated by electricity, but other than this the scene had been unchanged for millennia. There were sheep in protected fields, and a herd of deer bounding away from the swift approach of the electric train.

"I didn't know it could be so beautiful," Sara said. "I've never been this far north before. But it seems so sterile and barren as well."

"It's really the opposite. Come in the summer and you'll find it bursting with life."

"Perhaps. Could I have a little more of that fascinating whiskey? It has my head spinning!"

"Keep it spinning. You'll sober up quickly enough in Inverness."

"I'm sure of that. You'll go directly to the hotel and wait for instructions. What about all this ski equipment?"

"I'll take half of it with me, check the rest in here at the left luggage."

"That sounds right." Sara sipped the malt whiskey and wrinkled her nose. "So strong. I'm still not sure I like it. Inverness is on the edge of the security area, you know. All hotel records are entered automatically into the police files."

"I didn't know. But I've stayed often enough at the Kingsmills so it won't appear out of the ordinary."

"No. You are fine, the perfect cover. But I don't dare appear on any records. And I don't think I'll be able to catch the last train back tonight. I'll have to stay in your room, if that's all right with you?"

"Absolutely delighted."

When she said this Jan experienced a delightful warming experience somewhere in the middle of his body. He remembered her breasts revealed so quickly in the café in London. He smiled unconsciously at the thought—and found her smiling back.

"You're terrible," she said, "just like all the other men." But there was more humor than anger in her words. "Instead of thinking about the dangerous business ahead I suppose that your hormone-drenched brain is thinking only of seducing me?"

"Well, not only that . . ."

They laughed together and Sara reached out and took his hand. "What you men never seem to understand," she said, "is that women can enjoy love and sex just as much as you can. Is it unladylike to admit that I have been thinking about you since that first disastrous night in the submarine?"

"Unladylike or not, I think it's wonderful."

"Very good," she said, all business again. "After you check in, go out for a walk, get some fresh air, or go drink in a pub. You'll pass me on the street and just tell me your room number without stopping. Then go to your room right after dinner. I don't want to hang about the streets too much after dark and I'll join you as soon as I find out what the plans are to be for tomorrow. Agreed?"

"Agreed."

Sara left the train before he did, vanishing in the crowd. Jan waved a porter over and had him bring the skiing gear to left luggage. It was a short walk to the hotel with his almost-empty pack on his back. Packs were more in use than suitcases in the Highlands at this time of year and it elicited no notice, even when he checked into the hotel.

"Welcome back, Engineer Kulozik, always a pleasure to see you. We are short on rooms so we can't give you your usual one. But there is a fine one on the third floor, if you don't mind."

"No problem," Jan said, taking the key. "Would you have the pack put in the room? I want to go out before the shops close."

"Our pleasure."

. . Everything went as planned. Sara nodded when she heard the room number and continued past him without stopping. He had an early meal in the grill and was in his room by seven. In the bookcase he found a John Buchan novel, almost required reading here, and he sat down with that and a weak whiskey and water. Without his realizing it the lost night's sleep caught up with him and the next thing he knew he was starting awake at the light tapping on the door. Sara slipped in quickly.

"Everything has been arranged," she said. "You will take the local train tomorrow to a station named Forsinard." She consulted a scrap of paper. "This is in the Achentoul Forest. Do you know it?"

"I know of it. And I have all the maps."

"Good. Emerge from the train with the other skiers, but look for a local man, very husky, with a black eyepatch. He is your contact. Follow him and he will take it from there."

"What will you do?"

"I'll be on the seven o'clock train south in the morning. There is nothing more I can do here."

"Oh, no!"

She smiled, with a warmth he had not seen before. "Turn off the lights and open the curtains. There is a beautiful full moon tonight."

He did, and it drenched the white landscape with an even paler light. Shadows, darkness, and snow. Jan turned at a sound and the moonlight fell on her body as well. The firm, round breasts he had glimpsed so briefly, her taut stomach, full hips, long thighs. Sara held her arms out and he gathered her to him.

Twelve

"We're not going to get much sleep this way," he said, tracing the contour of her arable breast with his finger, her outline still clearly visible in the moonlight from the window.

"I don't need much. And you'll have plenty of time for it after I leave. Your train's not until noon. Did I thank you yet for what you are doing to help rescue Uri?"

"Not in so many words—but there are other ways. Who is Uri that he is so important?"

"He is not important, not in himself anyway. It is what will happen if Security discovers who they have. His cover is an Italian seaman, and it is a good cover. But eventually they will discover that it is false. Then the interrogation will begin in earnest and there is no way to stop them from finding out he is an Israeli."

"Is that bad?"

"It would be disaster. Our country's international policy is one of strictly no contact, none whatsoever except through official channels. Some of us in external security don't see it the same way. We have to know what is happening in the outside world to protect our own nation. And once we discovered what life is like here it was hard to remain neutral. So, despite all orders to not get involved, despite the logical reason-

ing that any involvement is a threat to our homeland—
we *are* involved. It is impossible just to stand by and
do nothing."

"I've been standing by, doing nothing all of my
life."

"You didn't know," Sara said, putting her finger
to his lips to silence him, moving the warm length of
her body against his. "And you are doing something
now."

"Oh yes, I certainly am!" he whispered, gathering
her in his arms. He silenced her laughter with his lips.

Jan was awake later when she dressed and left,
but there was nothing for either of them to say. He
did not think he would be able to sleep after that, but
he did. It was full daylight when he awoke and he
was ravenous. The breakfast did justice to the Highland cuisine, the smoked kipper was a thing of joy,
and he was feeling remarkably fit, whistling while he
dressed. Since arriving in Scotland it had been more
like a holiday than a hurried attempt to save a man's
life. Perhaps save an entire country. These were just
words, the reality had not sunk in yet.

Nor did the trip on the clanking train do anything
to change the way he felt. There were a few locals
aboard, but the majority of the passengers seemed to
be skiers on holiday, filling the coaches with bright
clothes and laughter, bottles passing from hand to
hand. One thing, he certainly would not be noticed in
this crowd. With people getting off and on at each station there would be no trace of where he had actually
alighted.

By midafternoon the sky had darkened and a thin
snow had begun to fall. This dampened feelings some-
what and, when he lifted the packs and skis down
from the guard's van in Forsinard, the bite of the

wind drove the last traces of merriment from him. This desperate business was about to begin.

His contact was easy enough to spot, a dark blob among the colourful anoraks and salopettes. Jan dropped his burden into the snow and knelt to fumble with the lace on his boot. When he arose again he went back in the direction of the station, following the stocky form of his contact. Along the road, then off onto a beaten down path through the trees. The man was waiting in a clearing well hidden from sight of the road.

"What do I call you?" he said when Jan came up. "Bill."

"Well, Bill, I'm Brackley, and that's no code name and I don't care who knows it. I've done my time and left an eye behind to prove it." He pointed to the black patch and Jan noticed the puckered scar that crossed his cheek and went under the patch, continuing up over his forehead and vanishing under the wool cap pulled low on his head. "They've been trying to do old Brackley for years but they haven't done me so far. You cold?"

"Not very."

"Good. Make no difference if you were. Be dark before the track comes. What do you know about the work camps?"

"Little or nothing. Other than the fact that they exist."

Brackley snorted and nodded at the answer, then extracted a plug of tobacco from his pocket and bit off a corner. "That's the way they want it," he said indistinctly around the large cud he was chewing into shape. "What happens, people get out of line, they get sent up here, maybe a ten-year sentence cutting trees. Good for the health unless you cross the screws, then you get this," he jerked his thumb at the eyepatch again, "or worse. Dead too, they don't care. Then

111

when you serve your term you find out that you got to serve the same term again working in the Highlands, no going back to the joys of the Smoke. And there ain't no work here. Except grazing sheep. You people, begging your pardon, your honor, likes their little bit of meat, don't they. Poor buggers up here freezing their arses off to see you get it. So what with ten years inside and ten years with the sheep, most don't get back south, and them what do, they keep their noses clean so they can stay south. It's a good system they got, works fine." He spat a great brown gob into the white snow.

"What about escapes?" Jan asked, stamping his feet as the cold began to seep through.

"Easy enough to get out. Couple of strands of barbed wire. But then what? Wilderness on all sides, a few roads well watched, trains watched as well. Getting out's no problem, staying out is the one that counts. That's where Brackley and his boys come in. All of us done our time, now we're out but can't leave the Highlands. So while we're here we don't make trouble, but anyone goes through the fence and finds us, why we make trouble for the screws. Get them out of here. South. Like an underground railway. Turn them over to your people. Now you want one out in particular, right out of a security cell. Not easy."

"I don't know the details."

"I do. First time you've given us guns. This could stop other things working around here for a long time. Once we have this man out we go back to our crofts and lay low for a long time. Raise our heads we get 'em cut off. This man better be important."

"He is."

"That's the way I hear it. So let's look at the map before it gets too dark. Here's where we are now." He pointed out the spot with a thick, scarred thumb. "We start cross country after dark to about here, doesn't

112

show on the map but that's their detector screen. Go in on foot after that and they can't tell us from elk or deer. Not that they care. Only start looking after someone breaks out. No one up until now has been fool enough to want to break in. We use snowshoes. We want to use these fancy skis of yours?"

"Yes, they're best for me."

"Good enough. We'll bring the man out in a ski-basket so we can make time. Back to the track, back to the road, run the track into a lake, and we go home and no one the wiser."

"Aren't you forgetting something?"

"Never!" He slapped Jan on the back, a friendly blow that sent him staggering. "Right along here there are a number of paths where the skiers cross the road. Even if it's not snowing they'll never be able to follow your tracks—they go every which way from here. You and your friend break west then and you'll have at least eight, ten hours of darkness to stay ahead of anyone looking for you. Not that they will, probably won't think of it. They'll look for someone going to ground, or going north or south by train or road. This is a new way out and a smart one too. You'll get through, though there will be mobile patrols around when you get over near Loch Naver."

"We'll look out for them."

"That's the spirit." Brackley squinted up at the darkening sky, then took up the second pack and pair of skis. "Time to go."

Jan was thoroughly chilled through now, standing in the patch of pine trees by the road, as the dark afternoon thickened into night. Invisible snowflakes melted on his face and he moved stiffly when Brackley pulled him forward at the sight of twin headlights coming slowly along the road. A dark vehicle stopped and a door swung open above them, ready hands pulled them inside.

"Lads, this is Bill," Brackley said, and there was a murmur of greeting from the unseen men. His elbow dug Jan painfully in the ribs, to draw his attention. "This is a snowtrack. He nicked it from the foresters. Can't do it too often because they get right annoyed and turn the whole county over. They'll be annoyed again in the spring when they find it sunk in the lake. Had to do it this time. For speed."

There was a heater on in the body of the vehicle and Jan thawed out a bit. Brackley produced a torch and held it while Jan took off his boots, massaging some life back into his icy feet, then put on high socks and the special cross-country shoes. He was still tying the laces when they lurched to a stop.

They seemed to know just what to do without being told, since no orders were issued. The men piled out of the track into waist high snow, quickly strapping their feet into the round bear-paw snowshoes. The first two men were already away, towing the mountain rescue stretcher on its skis. There was white official lettering stenciled on it, also undoubtedly stolen. Jan strapped on his skis and kicked off quickly after them through the trees, wondering how they could find their way in the snow-filled darkness.

"Hold it," Brackley said, stopping so suddenly that Jan almost ran into him. "This is as far as you go. Take this and wait here." He pressed the bulk of an FM transceiver into Jan's hands. "If anyone comes by and sees the cut wire, don't let them see you. Get back into the trees. Press this button and tell us on the radio so we can come back a different way. Then get further back into the woods and we'll use the radio to find you."

There were some sharp metallic clicks as the barbed wire strands were cut, then silence. Jan was alone.

Very much alone. The snow had stopped but the

night was still dark, the moon concealed by thick cloud. The posts and barbed wire vanished away into the darkness on both sides; their presence was marked by the cleared strip of land. Jan slid away to the shelter of the trees, moving back and forth there to keep warm, checking the glowing digits on his watch. A half an hour and still nothing. He wondered how far they had to go, how long it would all take.

By the time a slow hour had dragged by his nerves were tightened to the snapping point. At one point he jumped with shock, almost falling as dark shapes moved out of the trees toward him. Deer. Far more frightened than he was once they caught his scent. After almost ninety minutes more dark shapes appeared, and he almost thumbed on his radio, before he recognized the stretcher being towed behind them.

"Went just wonderful," Brackley said hoarsely, panting for air. They had all been running. "Didn't need the guns, used the knives and did away with a half-dozen of the bastards. Got your friend here all right, though they've knocked him about a bit. Here, take the rope and pull the litter, my lads are fair bushed."

Jan grabbed the rope and passed it over his shoulder, tying it to his belt, then leaned his weight into it. The stretcher moved easily on its skis and he broke into a steady, loping run that quickly caught up and passed the others on their snowshoes. He had to slow then to stay behind Brackley who was leading the way. Short minutes later they were back in the snowtrack and passing the stretcher in over the tailgate. The fuel cell fired with a muffled roar and they started forward even as the last of the men were climbing aboard.

"We have a half an hour at least, maybe an hour," Brackley said, drinking deep from the water bottle, then passing it along. "All the guards at the detention cells are dead—the roof will blow off that place when they're discovered."

"But they got other things to think about," one of the men broke in; there were murmurs of agreement at that.

"We set fire to some of the warehouses," Brackley said. "That will keep the bastards distracted for a bit."

"Would someone be so kind as to unstrap me?" the man in the stretcher said.

A light flashed on and Jan undid the straps that held Uri secure. He looked young, perhaps still in his twenties, with black hair and deepset dark eyes.

"Can anyone tell me what happens next?" he asked.

"You're going with me," Jan said. "Do you know how to ski?"

"Not on snow, but I water ski."

"That's very good. We won't be doing downhill skiing, but cross country. I have the clothes here that you will need."

"Sounds like fun," Uri said, sitting up, shivering. He was dressed only in a thin gray prison uniform. "I'll sit on the bench if someone will give me a hand."

"Why?" Jan asked, struck by a sudden cold sensation of fear.

"Bunch of bastards back there," Uri said, dropping to the bench. "Thought I wasn't talking fast enough, even when they got an Italian translator in. They used some encouragement to speed me up."

He lifted his foot from the tangled blankets. It was dark with dried blood. Jan leaned close with the light and saw that all of the man's toenails had been ripped out. How was he to walk—much less ski—with feet like this?

"I don't know if it helps," Brackley said. "But the people who did this, they're all dead."

"It doesn't help the feet but it cheers me a great deal. Thank you."

"And we'll take care of the feet too. There was always a chance something like this might happen." Brackley struggled a flat metal container out from under his clothing and opened it. He took out a disposable syringe and broke off the safety tip. "People who gave me this said one shot would kill pain for up to six hours. No side effects but very habit forming." He slapped it against Uri's thigh, the sharp needle penetrating the thin fabric, the drug slowly injected by the pressurized gas capsule. "There are nine more here." He passed them over.

"My thanks to whoever thought of this," Uri said. "The toes are getting numb already."

Jan helped him to dress in the swaying snowtrack. The lunging ride improved when they came to a road and speeded up. They only followed it for a few minutes, then turned off into the deep snow again.

"Security checkpoint ahead," Brackley said. "We have to go around it."

"I had no idea of your shoe size," Jan said. "So I bought three pairs of shoes, different sizes."

"Let me try them. I'll wad some bandages around the toes to soak up blood. I think these are the ones that will do."

"Do they fit well in the heel?"

"Fine." Dressed and warming up, Uri looked around at the circle of watching men, barely seen in the light of the torch. "I don't know how to thank you people . . ."

"You don't. Our pleasure," Brackley said as the vehicle slowed and stopped. Two of the men left in silence and the snowtrack started up again. "You two will be the last. I'll be driving and I'll take care of disposing of this thing. Bill, I'll drop you at the spot I

117

showed you on the map. After that you're on your own."

"I'll take care of it," Jan said.

Jan rearranged the packs, putting over three-quarters of the weight into the one he would carry, then adjusting the lighter one on Uri's shoulders.

"I can carry more than that," Uri said.

"On foot maybe, but if you can just carry yourself on skis I'll be happy. The weight's no problem for me."

The snowtrack was empty when they stopped for the last time. Brackley came around from the cab and opened the rear and they slid down to the icy surface of the road.

"That's the trail," Brackley said, pointing. "Get off the road fast and don't stop until you're under the trees. Good luck."

He was gone before Jan could phrase an answer. The snowtrack roared away, sending back a shower of broken bits of ice, and they were alone. Struggling through the thick snow to the trees. Uri held the small torch while Jan knelt and strapped his shoes into the skis, then put on his own.

"Slip the thong of the ski pole over your wrist like this, see. So the pole hangs from your wrist. Now move your hand straight down and grab. This way you can't lose a pole. Now here is the motion you will have to use, a sliding one. As you slide your right foot forward you push against the pole in your *left* hand. Then shift weight and push the opposite ski with the opposite pole. That's it, keep going."

"It's . . . not easy."

"It will be as soon as you get the rhythm right. Watch me. Push . . . push . . . Now you go ahead, follow those tracks, I'll be right behind you."

Uri struggled ahead and was just getting into the swing of the movements when the path turned off and they faced the soft powder snow of the deep forest. Jan went first then, striking a path through the unbroken surface. The sky was growing light above the black silhouettes of the trees and when they came to a clearing Jan stopped, looking up at the moon riding above the moving clouds. Clearly visible ahead was the grim shape of a mountain.

"Ben Griam Beg," Jan said. "We go around it . . ."

"Thank God! I thought you might want to take me over it." Uri was panting, drenched with sweat.

"No need. We'll hit frozen lakes and streams on the other side, going will be easier and we'll make better time."

"How far do we have to go?"

"About eighty kilometers as the crow flies, but we won't be able to get there directly."

"I don't think I can make it," Uri said, staring with misgivings at the frozen wilderness ahead. "Do you know about me, I mean were you told . . . ?"

"Sara told me everything, Uri."

"Good. I have a gun. If I can't make it you are to shoot me and go on. Do you understand?"

Jan hesitated—then slowly nodded.

Thirteen

They went on. They were stopping far oftener than Jan wanted to because Uri was not able to keep up a steady pace. But he was learning, going faster with less effort. They had only four more hours of darkness. At the next stop, around the shoulder of the mountain, Jan checked their heading with the gyrocompass and tried to mark his course with an indentifiable spot in the terrain ahead.

"Going . . . to have to have . . . another shot," Uri said.

"We'll take ten minutes then, something to eat and drink."

"Damn . . . fine idea."

Jan dug two dried fruit bars from his pack and they chewed on them, washed down with water from the insulated bottle.

"Better than the food inside," Uri said, wolfing his portion. "I was there three days, nothing much to eat, less to drink. It's a long way to *eretz* Israel. I didn't know there could be this much snow in the whole world. What's the plan when we finish this little holiday trek?"

"We're making for the Altnacealgach Hotel. It's a hunting lodge, right out in the forest by itself. I imagine you'll be picked up there, or perhaps I'm supposed to drive you someplace. My car will be there. In any case you will hide out in the forest a bit while I go ahead."

"I'm looking forward to your hotel. Shall we go on before I seize up and can't move."

Jan was tired himself well before dawn—and he did not want to think how Uri felt. Yet they had to keep moving, to get as much distance as they could from the camp. There had been some snow flurries during the night, not very heavy, but still thick enough he hoped to obscure their tracks. If Security would be looking for tracks. There was a good chance they wouldn't, not yet. But danger would come with sunrise; they had to be concealed before then.

"Time to stop," Jan called back over his shoulder. "We're going to ground over here, under the trees."

"Those are the most beautiful words I have ever heard."

Jan stamped out depressions in the snow and spread the sleeping bags out in them. "Get into yours," he ordered. "But take your shoes off first. I'll take care of them. And I'll get us some warm food."

He had to help with the shoes, saw the socks and bandages sodden with blood. "Good thing I can't feel anything," Uri said, sliding into the sleeping bag. Jan pushed snow over it until it was completely concealed.

"These bags are made of insulcon, fabric developed for space suits. It has a layer of insulating gas in it, almost as good a nonconductor as a vacuum. You'll find you'll have to leave the top loose or you'll stew in your own juice."

"I'm looking forward to it."

The light was growing now; Jan hurried with the food. The electric element on the high density battery quickly melted a potful of snow, into which he dumped a packet of dehydrated stew. A second potful heated while they wolfed down the first. Then Jan cleaned up, melted water to top up their bottles, then packed everything away again. It was full daylight. Well below the horizon an airplane droned by. The search would be on. He wriggled into his own sleeping bag and pulled snow over it. A long snore issued from Uri's bag. That sounded like a good idea. He set the alarm on his watch and pulled the flap over his face. At first he was afraid he would stay awake, worrying about the search that was going on, but sleep overwhelmed him and the next he knew the piercing warble of the alarm was screeching in his ear.

During the second night, even though the going was easier, they covered less distance than they had the previous one. Uri was losing blood, too much of it, and even with the pain-killing injections he found it harder and harder to go on. They crossed a frozen loch about an hour before dawn and came to a sheltered cove with an overhanging rock ledge. Jan decided to stop. The place was ideal and it wasn't worth the few kilometers more to force Uri any further.

"I'm not doing too well, am I?" Uri asked, sipping at a steaming mug of tea.

"You're turning into a good cross-country skier. Be winning medals soon."

"You know what I'm talking about. I don't think I'm going to get there."

"After a good sleep you'll feel better."

It was sometime in the afternoon when Uri's voice dragged Jan from a deep sleep. "That sound. Can you hear it? What is it?"

Jan lifted his head free of the sleeping bag, then heard it clearly. A distant whine, far down the loch.

"A snowcat," he said. "It sounds like it might be coming this way, along the loch. Keep your head down and he won't see us. Our tracks have filled in so he can't follow them."

"Is it the police?"

"Probably. I can't think of anyone other than the authorities who would be running mechanical equipment out here in the winter. Stay quiet, we'll be safe."

"No. When he gets close, sit up and wave, draw his attention."

"What? You can't mean it . . ."

"I do. I'm not getting out of these woods, not on foot. We both know that. But I can do it with transportation. Let him get as close as possible before you make your move."

"This is crazy."

"It is. This whole mess is crazy. There he comes."

The whining rose in volume as the snowcat came around a headland jutting into the loch. It was bright red, its spinning tread throwing a spume of snow behind it, the goggled rider looking straight ahead. He was paralleling the shore and would pass an easy ten meters from them. Concealed as they were, in the snow under the ledge, there was very little chance of his accidentally seeing them.

"*Now!*" Uri said, and Jan rose up out of the snow, waving his hands and shouting.

The rider saw him at once and throttled down, turning at the same time, swinging toward them. He reached down and unclipped his microphone and was raising it to his mouth when Uri's shot caught him in the chest. A shot from a rocket pistol. It fired a silent, self-propelling projectile that tore right through the man.

He went over backward, arms wide. The snowcat fell on its side, skidding forward, track churning, until the tumble switch cut the power.

Fast as Jan moved, Uri was faster. Out of his bag, his feet making red prints in the snow, rushing toward the fallen man. There was no need.

"Dead as soon as he was hit," Uri said, opening

the officer's jacket and peeling it from him. "Look at the hole that thing punched right through him." Uri wasted no time as he pulled on the man's clothing, stopping only to mop blood from the fabric. Jan walked over slowly and righted the snowcat.

"The radio is still switched off. He never sent a message," he said.

"Best news I have had since my bar mitzvah. Will I have any problem making that thing go?"

Jan shook his head *no*. "Almost a full charge in the battery, two hundred kilometers at least. The right handlebar is switch and throttle. They're fun to drive. The front steering ski will tend to go straight unless you lean your weight into the turn as well. Ever ride a motorcycle?"

"Plenty."

"Then you'll have no problems. Except where do you go?"

"I've been thinking about that." Dressed now in uniform and boots, Uri stamped over to their packs and took out the detailed map. "Can you show me where we are now?"

"Right here," Jan pointed. "At this inlet in Loch Shin."

"This town of Durness, on the north coast. Are there any other places in Scotland with the same name?"

"Not to my knowledge."

"Good. I had to memorize a list of towns with safe contacts in case of trouble. I have one there. Can I make it?"

"You'll make it if you don't run into trouble. Go this way, following the streams. That will keep you well away from these two north-south roads. Take a compass and follow this heading. Stay on it until you hit the coast. Then double back and lay-up in hiding until dark. Put on your own clothes and see if you can't drive the machine off the cliffs into the ocean—along with the uniform. After that—you're on your own."

"No problem then. But what about you?"

"I'll go on. Have a nice cross-country trek, something I enjoy. No worry about me."

"I didn't think so. But what about our friend the corpse here?"

Jan looked at the man's pink, bloodstained flesh, obscenely sprawled in the snow. "I'll take care of him. Cover him up back there in the forest. The foxes will find him, and then the crows. By spring there'll only be bones left. It's not very nice . . ."

"His job wasn't very nice. I'll appreciate it if you would take care of it. Then I can move out." He put out his gauntletted hand and Jan took it. "And I'm free thanks only to you and your people. We'll win, you wait and see."

"I hope so. Shalom."

"Thanks. But Shalom later. Let's get rid of the bastards first."

Uri twisted the control and moved off, faster and faster. He gave one last wave over his shoulder then was around the bend in the lake and gone, the sound of the electric motor dying away.

"Good luck," Jan said quietly, then turned back to their campsite.

The body first. He dragged it by its heels, arms sprawled over its head and a trail of blood marking its passage. The scavengers would be there as soon as he was gone. He kicked snow over the blood and went back to break camp. The second sleeping bag and all the extra equipment went into one pack, everything he would need into the other. There was no point in hanging about here, it would be dangerous in fact if the scene of the ambush were discovered. If he went through the forest carefully, he could be a good distance away before dark. Donning his pack, he grabbed up the other pack and the skis and went swiftly away from the site. It was good to move quickly and surely and the kilometers sped by. He buried the skis and pack in the middle of a dense thicket, then pressed on. Once he heard another snow-cat passing in the distance and he stopped until it had gone. A plane thrummed over head toward sunset, as invisible to him through the trees as he was to it. He went on two hours more before he made camp.

It snowed, heavily, during the night, and he woke up more than once to clear the drifts away so he could breathe. In the morning the sun burned golden-bright on the freshly fallen powder and he found himself whistling as he boiled the water for tea. It was over, all over, and he was safe. He hoped Uri was as well. Safe or dead, Jan knew that the Israeli would not be taken alive a second time.

When he crossed Benmore Loch it was late after-noon. He stopped and slid under the shelter of a tree when he heard the sound of a car going by on high-way 837 ahead. The hotel would not be far now. But what shoud he do? There would be no difficulty in spending another night in the snow, then going on in the morning. But would that be wise? If he were un-der any suspicion at any time the shorter the trip he had made the less chance there would be that he might have gone north to Slethill Camp before dou-bling back. So the best thing would be an early ar-rival. A steak dinner, with a bottle of wine, by an open fire was not a bad thing at all to look forward to.

Jan swung forward, moving swiftly, onto the slope behind the great hotel, then snowplowing down into the yard. He unstrapped his skis and stuck them into a drift by the front entrance. Then, kicking the snow from his shoes, he pushed through the double doors and into the lobby. It seemed hot and close after his days in the open.

As he walked across to the registration desk a man came out of the manager's office and turned toward him.

"Well, Jan," Thurgood-Smythe said. "Did you have an enjoyable journey?"

Fourteen

Jan stopped, eyes wide, stunned by the presence of his brother-in-law. "Smitty! What on earth are you doing here?" Only later did he realize that his natural response had been the right one; Thurgood-Smythe was studying his reaction closely.

"A number of reasons," the Security man said. "You're looking fit, clear-eyed, and glowing. How about a drink to put some toxins back into your body?"

"Fine idea. But not in the bar. Air's like treacle down here. We can drink just as well in my room—and I can crack the window a bit while you sit on the radiator."

"All right. I have your key here, save you the trouble. Let's go up."

There were others in the lift so they did not talk. Jan stared straight ahead and struggled to compose his thoughts. What did Thurgood-Smythe suspect? His presence here was no accident. Nor was he pretending that it was—not with Jan's key in his possession and making no secret of the fact. But a search would mean nothing: there was nothing incriminating in his luggage. Attack was the best defense and he knew better than to pretend stupidity to his brother-in-law. As soon as the door closed behind them he spoke.

"What's up, Smitty? And do me the favor of not pretending this is an innocent business—not with my key in your pocket. What's Security's interest in me?"

Thurgood-Smythe stood by the window, staring unseeingly at the white landscape. "I'll have a whiskey if you please, neat. A large one. The problem, my dear Jan, is that I don't believe in coincidence. My credulity is limited. And you have been too close to too many interesting things just once too often."

"Would you mind explaining that?"

"You know as well as I do. The incident in the Red Sea, the illegal computer tap in your laboratory."

"Means absolutely nothing. If you think I tried to drown myself for some reason you're the one in need of an analyst, not me. Which leaves us the laboratory—with how many employees?"

"Point taken," Thurgood-Smythe said. "Thank you." He sipped at the whiskey. Jan opened the window a hand's breadth and inhaled deeply of the cold air.

"Taken alone, these two incidents are meaningless. I only worry about them when I find you in the Highlands at this time. There has been a very serious incident at one of the nearby camps which means your presence here *could* be very suspicious."

"I don't see why." Jan's voice was cold, his face expressionless. "I ski up here two or three times, at least, every winter."

"I know you do, which is the only reason I am talking to you like this. If I were not married to your sister this interview would be entirely different. I would have a biomonitor in my pocket which would give me a readout on your heartbeat, muscle tension, respiration, and brainwaves. With this I would know if you were lying or not."

"Why should I lie? If you have one of these devices pull it out and look at it and see for yourself."

Jan's anger was real; he did not like the way the conversation was progressing.

"I don't. I had one in my hand before I left—but I put it back in the safe. Not because I like you, Jan—which I do. That has nothing to do with it. If you were anyone else I would be interrogating you now instead of talking to you. If I did that, sooner or later Elizabeth would hear about it and that would be the end of my marriage. Her protective instincts for her little brother go far beyond reason, and I do not wish to put them to the test of choosing between you or me. I have the uneasy sensation that it would probably be you."

"Smitty, for heaven's sake—what is this all about?"

"Let me finish first. Before I tell you what is happening I want to make it absolutely clear what is going to happen. I'm going home to Elizabeth and tell her that you have been put under surveillance by a different department of Security. This is true. I will also tell her that I can do nothing to prevent it—which is also true. What will happen in the future will depend upon what you do in the future. Up until now, until this moment, you are in the clear. Do you understand that?"

Jan nodded slowly. "Thanks, Smitty. You're putting yourself out on a limb for me, aren't you? I imagine your telling me about the surveillance is a dangerous thing for you to do?"

"It is. And I would appreciate the return of the favor by your discovering some aspect of the surveillance, then telephoning me and complaining about it."

"Will do. As soon as I get home. Now if you will tell me what I'm supposed to have done . . ."

"Not done—what you *could* have done." There was no warmth now in Thurgood-Smythe's voice, no give in his manner. This was the professional Security man that Jan had never seen before. "An Italian seaman escaped from a work camp up here. An item normally of little interest. But two things make it important. His escape was aided from the outside—and a number of guards were killed. Soon after this happened we had a report from the Italian authorities. The man does not exist."

"I don't understand . . ."

"Does not exist in *their* records. His documentation was forged, very professionally. Which means he is the citizen of another country, a foreign agent."

"He could be Italian."

"Possibly. But for other reasons I doubt that strongly."

"If not Italian—then what country?"

"I thought you might be able to tell me." His voice was quiet, soft as silk.

"How would I know?"

"You could have helped him escape, guided him through the forest, have him hiding out there right now."

This was so close to what he had planned that Jan felt the short hairs stirring on his neck. "I could—if you say so. But I didn't. I'll get out my map and show you where I've been. Then you tell me if I was near your mysterious escapee."

Thurgood-Smythe dismissed the thought with a wave of his hand. "No maps. If you are lying—or telling me the truth—there will be no evidence there."

"Why on earth should another country spy on us? I thought this was a world at peace."

"There is no such thing as peace—just modified forms of warfare."

"That's a rather cynical statement."

131

"Mine's a rather cynical profession."

Jan filled both glasses again and sat on the window ledge. Thurgood-Smythe retreated as far from the cold blast as he could.

"I don't think I like the things that you are telling me," Jan said. "All this murder and prisoners and surveillance machines. Does this kind of thing happen often? Why don't we hear about it?"

"You don't hear about it, dear brother, because you are not meant to hear about it. The world is a very nasty place and there is no cause to bother people with the sordid details."

"You're telling me that important events in the world are kept secret from people?"

"I'm telling you just that. And if you have never suspected it, then you are a bigger fool than I took you to be. People of your class *prefer* not to know, to let people like me take care of the dirty work for you. And look down upon us for it."

"That's not true, Smitty . . ."

"Isn't it?" There was a cutting edge to his voice. "What was it you just called me? Smitty? Did you ever call Ricardo de Torres—Ricky?"

Jan started to answer, but could not. It was true. Thurgood-Smythe was descended from generations of drab civil servants; Ricardo de Torres from titled, landed gentry. For long seconds Jan felt impaled on that look of cold hatred; then his brother-in-law turned away.

"How did you find me up here?" Jan asked, trying to change the subject.

"Don't pretend to be simple. The location of your car is in the motorway memories. Do you realize the extent of the computer files and programming?"

"I never thought about it. Big I suppose."

"Far bigger than you realize—and far better organized. There is no such thing as having too much memory. If Security wanted to—and we may—we could monitor every second of your life, have it all on record."

"That's stupid, impossible. You're in my territory now. No matter how much circuitry you have, no matter how much memory, there is no possible way you could run surveillance on everyone in the country all of the time. The data would swamp you."

"Of course it would. But I wasn't talking about the entire country. I was mentioning only one individual. You. Ninety-nine percent of the people in this country are neutral, neuters. Names in a memory bank of no interest to us. Proles who are identical as matchsticks. Society butterflies, who while richer and more exotic, are equally uninteresting. In reality, we have very little to do. Petty thievery and embezzling head our list of crimes. Of no real importance. So when we are asked to take interest in someone we do it with a vengeance. Your screen can be two-way—as can your phone. Your computer is accessible to us, no matter how secure you may think. Your auto, your laboratory, the mirror in your toilet, the light above your bed—are all in our employ . . ."

"You're exaggerating!"

"Perhaps. But not by much, not in reality. If we want to know about you we can easily know *all about you*. Don't ever doubt that. And we want to know about you now. I would say that, for a number of years—until your guilt or innocence is proven—this is the last private conversation that you will ever have."

"Are you trying to scare me?"

"I hope so. If you are involved in anything—get out. We'll never know, and I for one prefer it that way. But if your hands are soiled we are going to get you. Yes we will—as certain as the sun rises in the east."

Thurgood-Smythe crossed over to the door and opened it. He turned as though to add something, then thought better of it. He turned and left and the door closed heavily behind him.

Jan closed the window; he was getting chilled.

Fifteen

The only thing to do now was to appear normal—
try to act naturally in every way. Jan unpacked his
bag, knowing that Thurgood-Smythe had undoubtedly gone through it, apprehensive lest something incriminating had been slipped in by accident. There
was of course nothing; but he still could not displace
the niggle of fear. It stayed with him while he bathed
and changed, went down to dine, talked with old acquaintances in the bar. The feeling stayed with him
all night and he slept little. He checked out early the
next morning and began the long drive back to London.

It was snowing again, and he had no leisure to
think of anything else as he drove carefully down the
winding Highland roads. Luncheon was beer and a
pasty in a roadside pub, then on until he came to the
motorway. Once the computer took control he could
relax—but did not. He felt more uneasy if anything.

Sitting back, blinded by the torrent of snowflakes
against the window, yet completely safe under electronic control, Jan finally faced up to what was dis-
turbing him. There, right before him, was the evidence. The circle of tiny holes around the center of the
steering wheel. Monitoring his breath. He could not
drive and escape them. Inlets to an analyzer that de-

tected the parts per million of alcohol on his breath, that only permitted him to drive the car when he was legally sober. An intelligent idea to prevent accidents: an insinuating, humiliating idea when viewed as part of the bigger picture of continuous observation. This, and his other personal data, were stored in the car's memory, could be transmitted to the highway computer—and from there to the Security memory banks. A record of his breath, his drinking, his reaction time, where he drove, when he drove—whom he drove with. And when he went home the Security cameras in the garage and halls would follow him carefully to his front door—and beyond. While he watched TV the set would be watching back, an invisible policeman gazing out from the screen. His phone monitored, indetectable bugs planted in the wiring. Find and remove them—if possible—and his voice within the room would then be monitored by focusing a laser beam on the glass of his windows. Data and more data would be continuously fed to some hidden secret file—where all of the rest of the facts of his life were already recorded.

He had never thought seriously about it before, but he realized for the first time that he existed as two people. The flesh and blood person, and the duplicate electronic file. His birth had been recorded as well as all pertinent medical information. His education, his dental record, financial record, and purchases. What books he bought, what presents he gave. Was it all on file someplace? With a sinking feeling he realized that it probably was. There was physically almost no limit to the amount of information that could be stored in the new molecular memory cores. Molecules flipped one way or another to record bits, bits forming bytes, bytes forming words and numbers. More and more and more. An encyclopedia in a piece of material the size of a pinhead, a man's entire life in a pebble.

And nothing he could do about it. He had tried, done his bit for the resistance, helped in a small way. But now it was over. Raise his head and it would be chopped off. Life wasn't that bad. Be glad he wasn't a prole, condemned to that existence for all the days of his years.

Must he stop? Couldn't it be changed? But even as the rebellious thoughts possessed him he realized that his heartbeat had increased, the muscles in his arm tensed as he made an inadvertent fist. Physiological changes that could be monitored, observed, considered.

He was a prisoner in an invisible cell. Make one step out of it and it would be the end. For the first time in his life he had the realization what freedom was, what he did not have. What lack of liberty was really about.

The drive home was dull and uneventful. The weather improved, when he passed Carlyle the snowstorm had ended and he drove under leaden skies. There was a play on the fifth channel and he turned it on but did not watch it; his head was too filled with the turbulence of his thoughts. Now that he could no longer take part in the resistance he realized how important it had become to him. A way to work for something he had come to believe in, to expiate the guilt he was just learning to feel. All over. By the time he reached home he was in the darkest of moods, scowling at the innocent lift attendant and slamming through his front door. He locked it and turned on the lights—and the bulb in the one important lamp did not come on.

So quickly? Someone had been in the flat while he was away.

He was innocent, he had to keep thinking that, innocent. And they could be watching him right now. Jan looked around slowly; nothing visible of course. He tried the windows, one by one, but all were closed and locked. Then he went to his wall safe and pressed the combination, flipped through the papers and cash inside. Everything looked in order. If Security had been here—it *had* to be them—they would surely have found his simple alarm system. Having it wasn't illegal, in fact it was a precaution most of his friends used. Now, there must be a natural reaction. He went to the phone, looking as angry as he felt, and called Building Management.

"Entered while you were away, sir? We have no record of any maintenance or emergency people going in during your absence."

"Burglars, thieves then. I thought you had security in this building?"

"We do, sir, the best. I'll check the recordings at once. Is anything missing?"

"Nothing that I can see after a quick look around, nothing important." He realized that he was looking at the TV while he talked, noticing the marks on the rug. "There is something, I just noticed. The TV has been moved. Perhaps they tried to steal it."

"There is that possibility. I'll report it to the police—and send up the mechanic to change the combination on your front door lock."

"Do that. Now. I'm not happy about this."

"Nor should you be, sir. A complete investigation will be made."

How subtle they were, Jan thought. Could the TV have been left off the marks on the rug on purpose? Was this a warning, a slight nudge in the ribs? He didn't know. But now that he had seen the moved set, reported it, he had to investigate further. If he were innocent that is what he would do.

He rubbed his jaw as he walked around the set. Then knelt to look at the screws that held the back in place. One of them had a fresh shine where a screwdriver had recently cut the surface. They had been inside it!

Within ten minutes he had the back off, the guts pulled, the circuit boards out—and was looking at the device wired across the power leads on one of them. It was the size of an acorn and shaped very much like one, with a glint of crystal in the rounded end. It had lined up with a tiny hole drilled in the front panel. Bugged! With a sharp movement he pulled it loose and bounced it in his palm angrily, making up his mind what to do next, what he would do if he were as innocent as he pretended to be. He went to the phone and called Thurgood-Smythe at home. His sister answered.

"Jan, darling, it's been ages! If you're free tomorrow . . ."

"Sorry, Liz, all tied up. And it was Smitty I wanted to talk to in any case."

"And not a word for your sister I suppose?" She pushed her hair back with her hand and tried to look martyred, but did not succeed very well.

"I'm a beast, Liz, you've always known that. But I'm in a rush now. We'll get together next week, I promise."

"You better. There's the sweetest girl I want you to meet."

"Lovely." He sighed heavily. "Now would you kindly put me through to your husband."

"Of course. Wednesday at eight." She blew him a kiss and touched the transfer button. An instant later Thurgood-Smythe was on the screen.

"Someone broke into my apartment while I was away," Jan said.

"Petty crime is getting very bad this winter. But

not my department, as you must know. I'll transfer this to the police . . ."

"Perhaps it *is* your department. Nothing was stolen but I found this wired to the TV." He held it up. "Very compact, very expensive. I haven't looked inside it but I imagine it has full sound video and broadcasts a signal for at least a kilometer. If it doesn't belong to your people it is certainly something you would want to know about."

"Indeed it is. I'll look into it at once. Are you involved in anything the industrial espionage people might have an interest in?"

"No. Communication satellite work."

"Then it is mysterious. I'll have that gadget picked up and let you know."

Jan had just finished putting the back on the set when the door annunciator chimed. A heavy-built man with a somber expression stood outside and produced a Security identification which he held before the camera when asked.

"That was quick," Jan said, letting him in.

"You have something for me?" the man said, tonelessly.

"Yes, here it is."

The Security man pocketed the bug without looking at it. He was staring at Jan instead, coldly. "Don't mention this to Mr. Thurgood-Smythe again," he said.

"What do you mean? What are you talking about?"

"I mean exactly what I said. The matter is out of your brother-in-law's hands because of the family relationship." He turned to leave and Jan called after him, angrily.

"You can't just walk out after saying that kind of thing. Who are you to order me about? What is the meaning of this bug?"

"You tell me," the man said, turning about

sharply. "Are you guilty of anything? Do you have a statement to make?"

Jan felt the color rising in his face. "Get out," he finally said. "Get out and don't bother me again. I don't know what this is about and I don't care. Just go away and stay away."

The door closed and it was the door of a cage. Jan was locked in and they were watching him from the outside.

During the day the circuitry work occupied his mind. He buried himself in the communication satellites—much to the pleasure of Sonia Amariglio—working hard to distract his thoughts. He was usually the last one to leave at night. Tired, and very glad that he was. A few drinks at the bar, sometimes even eating dinner there, staying on until he was tired enough to go home and to bed. It was foolish of him—he knew that surveillance could work as well any place—but he detested the idea that they were watching and listening in his own flat. Nor did he bother to search for any of the devices. That would be a fool's game. Better to imagine that he was being watched at all times and act accordingly.

It was the following Wednesday morning when his brother-in-law phoned him in the laboratory.

"Morning, Jan. Elizabeth asked me to call you."

The silence stretched as Jan waited. Thurgood-Smythe was silent as well, watching. It was obvious that nothing more was going to be said about Security.

"How is Liz?" Jan finally answered. "What's up?"

"Dinner tonight. She was afraid you would forget."

"I didn't forget. But I just won't be able to make it. I was going to call with my apologies . . ."

141

"Too late. There's someone else coming and it would be impossible to cancel now. Too embarrassing for her."

"Oh, God. She did say something about another of her girls! You couldn't . . ."

"Not easily. Better take your medicine. From the way she talks this one is really something different. From Ireland, Dublin, all the charm of the Gael and the beauty and so forth."

"Stop—I've heard it often enough in the past. See you at eight."

Jan broke the connection first, a feeble gesture that made him feel better.He *had* forgotten the damn dinner. If he had called earlier he could have gotten out of it—but not on the same day. Liz would be too unbearable. In fact it might be a good idea to go. Get a decent meal for a change—the food in the bar was giving him indigestion. And it wouldn't hurt Security to be reminded whom he was related to. And the girl might be presentable, though Liz's choices usually weren't. Social connections were more important to her than grace of form, and she had trotted out some diabolical women.

He left work early in the afternoon and mixed a drink for himself at home, soaking some of the tension out in a hot bath, then changing into a good suit. Liz would be looking daggers through him all night if he wore the shabby jacket he used for the office. She might even burn his food. It was best to stay on Liz's best side for peace of life.

The Thurgood-Smythes had a Georgian house in Barnet and the drive made Jan feel better. The countryside was attractive under the waning moon, silver and black and hard. Though it was already March, the winter showed no sign of loosening its grip. All of the lights in the front of the house appeared to be on, but there was only one car in the drive. Well, he would smile and be polite. And at least the food would be good. And he ought to play a few games of snooker with his brother-in-law, whether he wanted to be with him or not. The past was gone. The present and the future had to be innocent.

There was the sound of female laughter from the drawing room and Thurgood-Smythe rolled his eyes as he took Jan's coat. "Elizabeth has made a mistake this time," he said. "This one is actually bearable to look at."

"Thank God for small blessings. I can hardly wait."

"Is it going to be whiskey?"

"Please. Malt."

He put his gloves inside his fur hat and dropped them onto the table, then gave his hair a quick comb in the mirror. There was more laughter and the clink of glasses and he followed the sound. Thurgood-Smythe was bent over the drinks trolley. Elizabeth waved to him and the other woman on the sofa turned toward him and smiled.

It was Sara.

Sixteen

It took all of Jan's will, all of his years of practice at school in not showing emotion, to stop himself from letting his jaw hang or from popping his eyes. "Hello, Liz," he said, in what was definitely not his normal voice, and walked around the couch to kiss her on the cheek. She hugged him to her.

"Darling, so wonderful to see you. I've even made you a special meal, you'll see."

Thurgood-Smythe passed him a drink in a natural way, then refreshed his own. Didn't they know? Was this a farce—or a trap? He finally let himself look at Sara who was sitting demurely, knees together, sipping a small sherry. Her dress was long and dark green, with an old-fashioned look, a gold brooch at her throat the only jewelry.

"Jan, I want you to meet Orla Mountcharles. From Dublin. We went to the same school, not at the same time of course. Now we belong to the same bridge club and I couldn't resist bringing her home so we could chat some more. I knew you wouldn't mind, isn't that right?"

"My pleasure. You've a treat in store, Miss Mountcharles, if you've never tasted Liz's cooking before."

"Orla, please, we're not too formal at home."

There was a touch of Irish accent to her voice. She smiled at him warmly, then sipped delicately at her sherry. He desperately drank half the whiskey in a gulp and started coughing.

"Sorry, not enough water?" Thurgood-Smythe asked, hurrying over with the jug.

"Please," Jan gasped. "Sorry about that."

"You're just out of training. Have another one and I'll show you the new cloth on the snooker table."

"Finally replaced. It would have had value as an antique in a few more years."

"Indeed. But you can roll into the top pocket now, you don't need to pot with force to get over that ripple."

It was easy to chat like that, to turn away and follow to the billiard room. What was she doing here? What was this madness?

Dinner was not the trial he thought it would be. The food—as always—was wonderful, beef Wellington with four kinds of vegetables. Sara was demure and quiet, and talking with her was like playing a role on stage. He hadn't realized how much he had missed her, how empty he had felt when he knew that he would never see her again. Yet here she was—in the heart of Security. There was an explanation, of course, but he did not dare ask it. The talk was light, the food, and brandy after, very good. He even managed to play snooker and beat Thurgood-Smythe two games out of three.

"Too good for me," his brother-in-law said.

"Don't apologize—just pay up the five quid you owe me."

"Did we really agree on a fiver a game? All right, you're correct of course. Better than usual, our little Irish colleen."

"Better! Smashing is the word. Where on earth did Liz ever find one like this?"

"The bridge club, she said. I may take the game up myself if this is what the players look like."

"Well don't let on to Liz or she'll be insufferable and she'll be throwing a new one at my head every night."

"Settle for this one, you could do a lot worse."

"I might very well do that."

There was no hint of duplicity or hidden motives in Thurgood-Smythe's voice. The Security officer seemed far away. Could it be true, Jan kept asking himself. Has she really been accepted as an Irish girl? Then, perhaps she is one. He must know.

"It's starting to snow again," Sara said later, as they were getting their coats. "I do hate to drive in the snow."

Liz impaled Jan with the sternest of looks while her husband, in the background, rolled his eyes heavenward and grinned.

"The roads aren't bad yet," Jan said weakly.

"But they'll only get *worse*," Liz insisted, and went so far as to jab her elbow into his ribs when Sara faced away. "This is no night for a girl to drive alone." Her gaze, when it rested on Jan, would have frozen a pail of water.

"No, of course you're right," he hurried to say. "Orla, perhaps I can drive you?"

"I don't want to take you out of your way . . ."

"Not a problem," Thurgood-Smythe said. "He's no more than five minutes from the West End. And I'll have one of my drivers bring the car around to your club in the morning."

"Then it is all set," Liz said, smiling her warmest. "So you needn't worry about the drive at all."

Jan made his good-byes, kissed his sister affectionately, then went to get the car. While the heater took the chill off the interior he scrawled a quick note and palmed it. Sara was waiting at the front door and he held the door open for her, handing her the note as she came in. She had just enough time to read the two words there before the courtesy light went out. CAR BUGGED. As soon as they were out of sight of the house she nodded agreement.

"Where can I take you, Orla?" he asked.

"I really am sorry to make you go out of your way. It's the Irish Club in Belgravia, a bit of the ould sod abroad as people say. I always stay there when I'm in London. It's not really grand, but very homey. With a friendly little bar. They do a lovely hot whiskey, Irish whiskey of course."

"Of course. I can't say I ever had any."

"Then you must try. You will come in, won't you? Just for a few minutes. It's really not late yet."

This innocent invitation was driven home by a firm nod of her head and a slow and languid wink.

"Well, perhaps for a few minutes. It's nice of you to ask."

The conversation continued in this same light vein as he drove down the nearly empty Finchley Road and into Marble Arch. She gave him instructions; the club was easy enough to find. He parked just in front of the entrance and they entered, brushing melting snow from their coats. Except for one other couple they had the bar to themselves. While the waitress took the drink order Sara wrote on the back of the note he had given her earlier. He looked at it as soon as the girl turned away.

STILL SOUND BUGGED. ACCEPT INVITATION TO COME TO MY ROOM. LEAVE *ALL* YOUR CLOTHES IN BATHROOM THERE.

He raised his eyebrows high at the invitation and Sara smiled and stuck her tongue out at him in mock anger. While they talked he shredded the note in his pocket.

The hot whiskies were very good, their play-acting seduction even better. No, he didn't think her bold, yes people would misunderstand if they went to the room together. Right, he would go first with the key and leave the door unlocked.

In her room the curtains were closed and the bed turned back temptingly. He undressed in the bathroom as he had been instructed and found a heavy terry cloth bathrobe behind the door which he put on. Sara came in and he heard her lock the hall door. She had her fingers to her lips when he came out, and did not talk until she had closed the bathroom door behind him and turned on the radio.

"Sit down here and keep your voice low. You know that you are under Security surveillance?"

"Yes, of course."

"Then your clothes are undoubtedly bugged. But we're safe enough away from them. The Irish are very proud of their independence and this club is swept and debugged daily. Security gave up years ago. They lost so many devices that they were supplying the Irish intelligence services with all they needed."

"Then tell me quickly—what happened to Uri?"

"He's safe, and out of the country. Thanks to you."

She pulled him close and hugged him, giving him a warm and lingering kiss. But when his arms went around her as well she wriggled free and sat on the edge of the bed.

"Take the armchair," she said. "We need to talk. First."

"Well, as long as you say first. Would you start by telling me just who you are and how Orla got into my sister's house."

"It's the best cover we have, so I don't jeopardize it by using it too often. We've done a lot of favors for the Irish government; this is something they've done in return. Absolutely solid identification, birth, school records, the lot. All with my fingerprints and details. It was when we were running your records through the computer to see how to contact you again that the bells began to ring. Orla Mountcharles *did* go to Roedean, some years after your sister. The rest was easy. I boned up on the school, saw some friends of friends of friends, and was invited to join the bridge club. The rest was as natural as the law of gravity."

"I know! Expose Liz to a new girl in town, hopefully with fairly good looks, but preferably with good connections, and the trap is instantly sprung. Home and dinner with little brother. But isn't it damn risky with the keen nose of Thurgood-Smythe sniffing the air?"

"I don't think it sniffs quite as well in the cloister of his own home. This is really the safest way."

"If you say so. But what makes you think my clothes are bugged?"

"Experience. The Irish have a lovely collection of intelligence devices. Security builds them into belt buckles, pens, the metal spines of notebooks, anything. They don't broadcast but record digitally on a molecular level to be played back later. Virtually indetectable without taking to pieces every item you possess. Best to think you are bugged at all times. I only hope your body is still all right."

"Want to find out?"

"That is *not* what I meant. Have you had any surgery or dental work done since you came back from Scotland?"

"No, nothing."

"Then you must still be clean. They have put recording devices inside bridgework, even implanted them in bones. They are very skilled."

"This does very little for my morale." He pointed to the bottle of Malvern water on the nightstand. "You wouldn't have a drop of whiskey to go with that, would you?"

"I would. Irish, of course, Paddy's."

"I'm acquiring the taste."

He poured one for each of them, then dropped back into the deep chair. "I'm worried. As much as I love seeing you—I don't think there is anything more I can do for the resistance."

"It will be difficult, but not insurmountable. You remember I told you that you were the most vital man we had."

"Yes. But you didn't say why."

"Your work on the satellites. That means you have access to the orbiting stations."

"It does. In fact I have been putting off a trip for some time now. I have to examine one of the old comsats in situ, in space and in free fall. Everything will change when we bring it down to Earth, to the lab. Why is this important?"

"Because you can be a contact with the deep spacers. Through them we have opened lines of communication with a number of planets. Not perfect, but improving. And there is a revolt brewing already, the miners on Alpha Aurigae Two. They have a chance of success if we can get in contact with them again. But the government is aware that trouble is starting out there and Security has clamped a lid on everything. There is no way of getting a message to our people on the ships from Earth. You should be able to manage it on the station. We've worked out a way . . ."

"You're frowning," Jan said softly. "When you get all worked up like this you frown. You will get wrinkles if you keep it up."

"But I want to explain . . ."

"Can't it keep, just for a little bit?" he asked, taking her hands in his, bending to put his lips on her forehead.

"Of course it can. You are absolutely right. Come, cure my wrinkles," she said, pulling him down to her.

Seventeen

Sonia Amariglio was ecstatic next day when Jan told her that he felt it was time to examine the satellite in space.

"Marvelous!" she said, clapping her hands. "It just floats up there and no one has the intelligence to poke in the nose at the circuitry and see what has gone wrong. I get so angry I want to go myself."

"You should. A trip into space must be something to remember."

"Memories I would love to have. But this ancient machine does not run so well." She patted her ample bosom somewhere in the region of her heart. "The doctors say the acceleration would not be good for my tick-tock . . ."

"I'm so sorry. I'm being stupid, I didn't know."

"Please, Jan, do not apologize. As long as I stay out of spaceships they say I will live forever. It is enough that you will go—and will make a much better job of it. When can you leave?"

"I must finish the circuit that I'm in the middle of now, the multiresonant repeater. A week, ten days at the outside."

Sonia was sifting through the papers on her desk and extracted a gray UNOSA folder which she flipped through. "Yes, here it is. A shuttle for Satellite

Station leaving on March twentieth. I'll book you a place on it now."

"Very good." Very good indeed. This was the shuttle Sara had told him to be sure to be on, so that the schedules would mesh correctly.

Jan was whistling when he went back to work, a bit of "Sheep May Safely Graze." He became aware of the irony of the title and his present condition. He wasn't going to graze safely anymore—and he was glad of it. Ever since the beginning of surveillance he had been over-careful, walking on eggs. But no more of that. Seeing Sara, loving Sara, had put an end to that period of formless fear. He would not stop what he was doing just because they were watching him closely. It would make the work more difficult but it would not stop it. Not only would he work with the resistance, but he would do a little resisting on his own. As a specialist in microcircuits he was very interested in seeing just what sort of devices surveillance had come up with.

So far he had been unsuccessful. He had bought a new notebook to replace the one he had sawn open, then obtained a replacement ID card for the one inadvertently destroyed. Today it was the turn of his pen, the gold pen Liz had given him for Christmas. A good place for a bug since he usually had it with him. It was up his sleeve now, slipped there when he was pretty sure no optic pickups were on him. Now he would try a little skilled dissection.

A quick circuit check showed that the instrumentation on his bench was still bug free. When he had first started this unapproved research problem he had found out that his multimeter electron microscope and all of his electronic instruments were tapped and reporting to a small transmitter. After that he used the optical microscope, and saw to it that a short circuit of

4,000 volts went through the transmitter. It had vanished and not been replaced.

The pen disassembled easily enough and he examined each part carefully under the low power microscope. Nothing. And the drawn metal case looked too thin to hold any components; he put a few volts through it as well as a quick blast of radiation for the printed circuitry just in case he was wrong. He was about to reassemble it when he realized that he had not looked inside the ink refill.

It was messy but rewarding. He rolled the little cylinder about with the tip of one ink-stained finger. As thick as a grain of rice and perhaps twice as long. Using the micromanipulators he dissected it and marveled at the circuitry and electronics. Half of the bug was powerpack, but considering the minimal current drain, it should run six months at least without recharging. A pressure microphone that used all of the surface of the ink supply as a sound pickup, very ingenious. Discrimination circuits to ignore random noise and put the device in the recording mode only for sounds of the human voice. Molecule-level recorder. Transponder circuit that, when hit with the right frequency and signal, would broadcast the stored memory at high speed. A lot of work had gone into this, just to eavesdrop on him. Misapplied technology, which was the history of so much of technology. Jan wondered if the pen had been bugged before Liz had given it to him. Thurgood-Smythe might have arranged it easily enough. She had given him the same kind of pen for Christmas and he could have exchanged one for the other.

At this point the wonderful idea struck Jan. It might be a bit of bravado, a bit of hitting back—but he was going to do it no matter what. He bent to dissect the bug, carefully excising out the Read Only Memory section of the transponder. This was something he enjoyed doing. When it was finished to his satisfaction he straightened up and rubbed the knots from his back. Then called his sister.

"Liz—I have the greatest news. I'm going to the moon!"

"I rather thought you were calling to thank me for having that lovely little Irish girl to dinner."

"Yes, that too, very kind. I'll tell you all about her when I see you. But weren't you listening? I said the moon."

"I heard you. But, Jan, really, aren't people going there all of the time?"

"Of course. But haven't you ever wanted to go yourself?"

"Not particularly. It would be rather cold, I imagine."

"Yes, it would be. Particularly without a spacesuit. In any case it's not the moon I'm going to, but a satellite. And I think it's important, and so might Smitty, and I want to tell you all about it. I'll take you out for a celebratory dinner tonight."

"How thoughtful! But impossible. We have been invited to a reception."

"Then drinks, at your place. I'll save money. Six all right?"

"If you say so. But I don't understand all the rush . . ."

"Just boyish enthusiasm. See you at six."

Thurgood-Smythe did not return home until close to seven and Elizabeth showed very little interest in either satellites or space flight so, after exhausting the conversational possibilities of Orla, Jan turned his attention to mixing a large pitcher of cocktails. A new one called Death Valley, dry, hot, and deadly the bartender had explained, and leave out most of the tobasco for the ladies. Thurgood-Smythe arrived in a rush, puckered his lips over the cocktail, and listened

with half an ear to the satellite news. Which was undoubtedly old news to him if he were getting surveillance reports. Jan trailed after him, and had not the
slightest trouble in exchanging gold pens when his
brother-in-law changed jackets.

It would probably come to nothing, but there
was a certain sweet feeling of success to know he had
bugged the buggers. When he left they were relieved
to see him go.

On his way home he stopped at a twenty-four
hour shop and made the purchases as instructed. He
would be meeting Sara again later this same evening
and the instructions had been detailed and precise.

When he returned to his apartment he went
straight to the bathroom and extracted the tester from
the holder on his belt. He had done this, every day as
a matter of routine, since he had found the optic bug
set into the light fixture above the sink. Invasion of
privacy was one thing, sheer bad taste was another, he
had shouted as he had shorted the thing out. Since
that time some sort of unspoken arrangement seemed
to have been made. He made no attempt to search for
bugs in the rest of the apartment; surveillance, as far
as he could tell, kept their cameras out of the toilet. It
was still clear.

Running water into the tub should take care of
the sound bugs. There were so many ways of picking
up voices and sound that he did not even try to look
for them. Just mask them when needed. He bathed
quickly, with the water still running, toweled himself
dry, and dressed from the skin out with his recent purchases. Underclothes, socks, shoes, dark trousers—
roughly the color of the ones he had taken off—shirt
and sweater. All of his discarded clothing went into
the bag that had held the new items. He pulled on his
overcoat, buttoning it carefully to his chin, picked up
gloves and hat and left with the bundle of clothing.

With all of the bugs it might contain whirring and re-cording like mad.

He looked at the dashboard clock and slowed the car. He was to be at the rendezvous at nine precisely. No earlier and no later. It was a clear night and a few people were still about in the streets. He turned into the Edgeware Road and proceeded leisurely toward Little Venice. The radio was playing, a little louder than he usually liked it, but the music was also part of the arrangements.

It was exactly on the hour when he stopped at the bridge over Regent's Canal. A man walked out of the darkness and held the car door as he opened it. A scarf around his face concealed his identity. He eased the door shut, trying not to click the latch, then drove away. Jan's identity and bugs drove away too, along with his overcoat, shoes, and clothing. Until he was back in the car surveillance did not know where he was, could not see or hear him. A man waved to him from the towpath along the canal.

Jan followed about ten paces behind him, not trying to catch up. The wind was cold, cutting through the sweater, and he hunched his shoulders, hands jammed into his pockets. Their footsteps were soundless in the snow, the night quiet except for the sound of a television playing in the distance. The frozen canal was an unbroken layer of whiteness. They came to canal boats tied by the path. After look-ing around the leading man jumped aboard the sec-ond one and vanished from sight. Jan did the same, finding the rear door in the darkness and pushing it open. Someone closed it and the lights came on.

"Cold evening," Jan said, looking at the girl seated at the table. Her features were invisible behind the face-changer, but her hair and figure was un-doubtedly Sara's. The man he had followed in had a familiar smile and gap-toothed grin.

157

"Fryer," Jan said, wringing his hand strongly. "It's good to see you again."

"And yourself. Survived your little adventure I see, and did well in the bargain."

"We don't have much time," Sara said sternly. "And there is a lot to be done."

"Yes, m'am," Jan said. "Do you have a name or do I just keep calling you M'am like you were the Queen?"

"You may call me Queeny, my good man." There was mischief in her voice and Fryer caught it.

"Sounds like you two met before. So you, old son, we'll call you Kingy because I'm blowed if I remember what name you used last time. Now I have some good beer down in the bilge and I'll get it and we'll get on with the night's business."

They had just time enough for a warm embrace before Fryer clattered back up the stairs.

"Here you are," Fryer said, setting two heavy bottles on the deck. He dropped a metal box next to them and went to get a towel from the galley to wipe them dry. There were glasses ready on the table; Jan unscrewed one of the tops and poured them full.

"Home brew," Fryer said. "Better than the slops they serve in the pubs." He drained his glass in a single go and began opening the seals on the box while Jan poured him a second one. When the top came off Fryer lifted two small aluminum foil envelopes out of the box and set them on the table.

"To all appearances these are ordinary TV recordings," Sara said. "In fact you could play them on your set at home. One is an organ recital, the other a comedy program. Put them in the bag you will be taking with you—along with some recordings of your own. Make no attempt to hide them. Recordings like these are stock in trade with the spacers and there will be plenty about."

"Why are these so special?" Jan asked.

"Fryer, will you go on deck as a lookout?" Sara asked.

"That's the way, Queeny. What they don't know they can't tell."

He picked up the full bottle of beer and went out. As soon as the door closed Sara pulled off the face-changer and Jan had her in his arms, kissing her with a passion that surprised both of them.

"Not now, please, there is so little time," Sara said, trying to push him away.

"When will there be time? Tell me right now or I won't let you go."

"Jan—tomorrow then. Pick me up at the club and we'll go out for dinner."

"And for afters?"

"You know what you'll have for afters." She laughed and pulled away, sitting on the far side of the table from him.

"Maybe my sister is right," Jan said. "I might be the falling-in-love kind after all . . ."

"Please don't talk like that. Not now—or ever. There is only ten minutes before your car comes back, we must finish this."

He opened his mouth to speak—but did not. He nodded instead and she relaxed. But he noticed that she was wringing her fingers together, unknowingly. They would talk tomorrow. She pushed the recordings over to him.

"This is the important one, the organ recital," she said. "I don't know how it is done, but a computer memory has been worked into the background noise, the static."

"Of course! What an interesting idea. Any computer memory is composed of two signals, a yes and a no, that is all you have in binary. So a memory could be stretched out, modulated, changed in frequency, dropped in as apparently random bits of surface noise. And without the key no one else would be able to read it."

"I'm sure you're right. This is the way we have communicated in the past. But it is clumsy and slow and many of the recordings go astray. A new system has been worked out—and details are on this disk. This one *must* get through. The situation out there is ready to blow, and it will go up as soon as we can establish reliable communication. This will be just the beginning. Other planets will follow."

"All right," Jan said, putting the envelopes into his shirt pocket and buttoning the flap. "But why two of them?"

"Our contact on the deep spacer is sure he has been spotted, that the recording will be intercepted. So you will give the dummy to the first man that contacts you. Save the second for the real agent."

"How will I know what to do?"

"You will be watched. As soon as you are used to working in space you will be on your own. You will be contacted then. Whoever approaches you will use the phrase, 'Have you checked your safety line lately?' Give him the recording."

"The dummy?"

"Correct. The real agent will then come to you for the proper recording."

"It all sounds hideously complicated."

"It has to be. Just follow orders."

The cabin door creaked open slightly and Fryer spoke through the crack.

"Car coming in two minutes," he said. "Let's go."

Eighteen

In the beginning the shuttle trip was very much like a flight by normal jet. Jan had flown often enough for the novelty to have worn off. He had read most of the way across the Atlantic, and the only aerial view he had had of Cape Canaveral was of the tropical cloud bank that covered it. A ramp had sealed the jet to the terminal, and it was through another ramp that he had boarded the shuttle. Except for the lack of windows the interior was just like that of a normal aircraft. The TV screen before each passenger showed a reassuring meadow landscape, with nodding lilies and billowing white clouds, matched by the equally reassuring strains of Beethoven's "Pastoral." Liftoff, with a maximum of one and a half G acceleration was surely greater than a normal takeoff, but not of a surprising order. Even when the shielding had slipped back from the nose camera and a view of space had replaced the lilies, there was no great feeling of difference. It could have been just another TV program. Only when acceleration ceased completely and they were in free fall was the real change apparent. Despite the antinausea drugs the passengers had taken, the psychological effect was strong enough to affect a number of stomachs. The attendant was busy with the barfbags, and a hand-vacuum for the bits that missed the bags.

The reality of the occasion finally penetrated when a star ahead grew brighter, then took form. Satellite Station. A specialized satellite for space vehicles. Here the deep spacers came, ships built in the vacuum of space and destined never to enter a planet's atmosphere. They were served by stocky, winged shuttles like this one, vehicles that could land and take off from the planet below. There were spidery space tugs as well, skeletal ships that serviced the Earth satellites, repairing or replacing them as needed. This was the reason for Jan's presence here. A presence that would, hopefully, serve a dual purpose.

With quick blasts from its maneuvering jets the shuttle drifted toward the great bulk of the station, guided to final contact by computer control from the station itself. There was a slight tremor when they touched the contact pads, but no rebound as the magnetic grapples took hold. Short moments later the green light came on above the door and the steward spun the unlocking wheel. Five more uniformed men came aboard, kicking off easily and floating the length of the cabin, then grabbing the hand rails for graceful stops.

"Now you've seen them do it," the steward said. "But please don't try it yourself if you are not experienced. Most of you gentlemen have technical knowledge so you will know what I mean when I remind you that a body in free fall has no weight—but it still has mass. If you push off and hit the wall headfirst, you will feel as though you have hit the wall headfirst. So please remain seated as instructed, with your belts secured. The assistants will guide you out one at a time. Gently as though you were in your mother's arms."

While the steward was talking, four men in the

first rows unbelted and kicked themselves free. Experienced spacers by their movements. Jan knew better than to even try. He unlocked his belt when instructed, felt himself lifted and floated the length of the cabin.

"Grab the cable and don't let go until you reach the far end."

A rubbery endless cable emerged from a hole in the boarding tube's wall and moved steadily toward the station. A silvery panel on the tube must have had a weak magnetic field—there was undoubtedly an iron core to the cable—for the cable clung to the wall, sliding with an irritating squeaking sound. Yet it came away easily enough. Jan grabbed onto it and was towed the length of the tube, to the circular bay at the far end.

"Let go now," the man waiting there called out. "I'll guide you to a stop." He did it easily and swung Jan toward the rail to which his toes were hooked. "Do you think you can pull yourself hand-over-hand to that opening to the transfer room?"

"I can only try," Jan said, attempting the not too easy task. It worked well enough, though his legs did tend to float up over his head—if over were the right word. A ladder went down into the transfer room, leading to an open door. Four men were already in the small room beyond and the attendant closed the door as soon as Jan was in. The room began to move sideways.

"As we accelerate to match the station's rotation your weight will gradually return. The red wall will become the floor. Please orientate toward it so you will be able to stand on it."

As the spin increased so did their apparent weight. By the time the transfer room had matched the rotation speed of the station they stood solidly on a floor and waited for the attendant to open the hatch. Perfectly normal steps led downward into the station. Jan went first. The stairway led to a larger room with a number of exits. A tall, blond man was waiting there, looking at the new arrivals. He walked toward Jan.

"Engineer Kulozik?" he asked.

"That's right."

"I'm Kjell Norrvall." He put his hand out. "In charge of satellite maintenance. A pleasure to have you here."

"My pleasure. Getting into space."

"We're not exactly interstellar here—but we're still a long way from Earth. Look, I don't know if you're hungry or not, but I just came off shift and I'm starving."

"Give me a few minutes and I think I'll be able to eat. This going in and out of gravity isn't the easiest thing on the stomach."

"Neither is coming in on the wee-waw express with all the white bags . . ."

"Kjell, please . . ."

"Sorry. Change the subject. Good to see you here. First engineer from the London lab in over five years."

"It can't be."

"Certainly is. They sit there on their fat *balder*—present company excepted—and tell us what to do up here without the slightest idea of what our problems are. So you are welcome, I mean that. So you'll excuse my bad Norwegian jokes, yes?"

"Yes, of course. As soon as I settle down I'll make some myself."

"Right in here."

There was quiet background music in the dining room which had been decorated with some degree of taste. The flowers along the wall only looked like plastic when one came close. A few men were queuing at the self-service counter, but Jan had no desire to get that close to food quite yet.

"I'll find a table," he said.

"Can I get you anything?"

"Just a cup of tea."

"No problem."

Jan tried not to look too closely at the meal Kjell was wolfing with great enthusiasm; the tea went down very well and he was happy with that.

"When do I get to see the satellite?" Jan asked.

"As soon as we finish here, if you like. Your bag will be in your room waiting for you. Before I forget, here's the key, the number is on it. I'll show you how a spacesuit works and we can go out."

"Is it that easy—going into space?"

"Yes and no. The suits are about as foolproof as they can be made, so that's not a worry. And the only way to learn to work in zero-G in space is to go out and do it. You won't be flying, that takes a long time to learn, so I'll take you out in a powered suit and anchor you. Bring you back the same way. You can work as long as you want, to get the hang of tool using, then shout into the radio when you've had enough. You'll never be out there alone. One of us will get to you within sixty seconds. Nothing to worry about."

Kjell pushed his plate away and started on a large and violently red sweet. Jan turned his eyes away. The fabric paneling on the walls was attractive.

"No windows," Jan said. "I haven't seen one since I arrived."

"You won't either—only one is in the control tower. We're in geosynchronous orbit here, where most of the satelllites are. Also right in the middle of a Van Allen belt. Plenty of radiation out there—but plenty of shielding too in these walls. The suits we use have heavy shielding as well, and even with that we don't go out during solar storms."

"What is the situation now?"

"Quiet. And it should stay that way. Ready?"

"Lead the way."

Everything that could be automated in the space-suits was—with multiple standby and fail-safe circuits. Internal temperature, oxygen demand, humidity controls were all computer controlled. As was the control input.

"You just talk to the suit," Kjell said. "Call it suit-control, tell it what you want, then say end suit control when you are finished. Like this." He lifted the bowllike helmet and spoke into it. "Suit control, give me a status report."

"Unoccupied, all internal controls off, oxygen tank full, batteries fully charged." The voice was mechanical, but clear.

"Are there specific commands or phrases?" Jan asked.

"No, just speak clearly and the discrimination circuits will sort out the command words and phrases. It'll query if there is any doubt, and repeat any commands before actuating them."

"Sounds simple enough—I hope it is. Shall we start?"

"Now's the time. Sit down and put your legs in here . . ."

It went easily and Jan had faith in the suit circuitry when it warned him that his right glove wasn't sealed completely. With the helmet in place he lumbered after Kjell into the airlock. His suit unwrinkled as the pressure dropped and when it hit zero the outer door automatically unlocked.

"Here we go," Kjell's voice said on the radio hookup, and pushed them out through the opening.

They were on the dark side of the station. Words had not prepared Jan for the sight of the stars, unmasked by any atmosphere or pictured on a screen.

There seemed to be too many of them, filling all of space. Varying in brightness and color. He knew the arctic sky at night—but that had only been a suggestion of the grandeur and beauty that filled space around him. Long minutes passed without his realizing it, until Kjell spoke.

"It always hits you like that. But the first time is special."

"Unbelievable!"

"And it's not going away—so we can get some work done now."

"Sorry."

"Don't be. I feel the same way."

Kjell jetted them to the comsat which was anchored to a spar. The bulk of a deep spacer was not far beyond. Some men were working on her hull and there was the sudden red flare of a laser welder. Seen in space, in its correct environment, the communication satellite was more impressive than it had ever looked in the sterile room on Earth. It was gouged and eroded by years of bombardment of microparticles. They clipped onto it and Jan pointed out the cover plates he wanted removed. He watched closely as Kjell used the counter-rotating powered screwdriver. Then he tried it himself, clumsily at first but with increasing skill. After an hour of this he found the fatigue creeping up so he stopped and they returned. He turned in soon after and slept very well indeed.

When they went out again during the next work period he had the metal recording envelopes in his pocket. It was very easy to slip them into the outer leg pocket of his suit.

By the third day he was working well and Kjell seemed satisfied with his progress.

"I'm going to leave you alone now. Shout if you need some help—I'll be inside that navsat there," he said.

"I hope not. I have these boards out where I can get prods to them so I'm all set for a while. Thanks for the help."

"More thanks to you. This equipment has been waiting years for your master's touch."

Jan must have been under constant observation—or his radio messages were being monitored. Probably both. He was still unshipping his monitor screen when a spacesuited figure moved out from behind the nearby spacer, drifting his way with skillful puffs of gas from his backpack. The man came close, stopped, then touched his helmet to Jan's. Their radios were off but the sound of his voice came clearly through the contacting surfaces.

"Have you checked your safety line lately?"

His features were invisible behind the mirrored helmet. Jan fumbled the recording out of his pocket and passed it through the beam of his work light. It was the correct one. The man took it from his hand and pushed off at the same instant, turning as he drifted away.

A second man appeared out of the darkness, moving fast, faster than Jan had ever seen one of the suits move before. It was on a collision course and he slammed into the first man with a soundless impact, triggering the laser welder he held before him just as they hit.

It was a microsecond burst, a jet of brilliant red light that burned a gaping hole through suit and man in an instant. Oxygen puffed out and froze into a cloud of tiny brilliant crystals. There was no radioed alarm either; the attacker must have placed the beam to destroy the suit computer as well.

Jan was still rigid with shock when the second man let the laser swing from its line and grabbed the dead man, triggering his jets at the same time. They must have had specially fitted high-pressure orifices

because the two figures accelerated away swiftly—
then separated. The attacker reversed thrust, but no
longer held onto the dead man. The corpse went out
and out, leaving a comet tail of frozen oxygen, growing smaller, dwindling from sight.

The other man braked to a stop next to Jan and
held his hand out. For a long moment Jan, still
shocked by the speed and deadliness of the attack, did
not realize what was needed. Then he reached into his
pocket and extracted the second recording, passing it
over. He could not help recoiling when the other helmet moved and pressed against his.

"Well done," the distant voice said.

Then he was gone.

Nineteen

Two days later, in the middle of a sleep period, Jan was woken by the shrill beep-beep of the phone. He blinked at the illuminated time readout; he had only been asleep about three hours. With a muttered grumble he turned on the phone and Sonia Amariglio's features filled the screen.

"Jan, are you there?" she said. "My screen's dark."

Still hoping to get back to sleep, he switched to infrared pickup instead of turning on the light. His image would be black and white, but clear enough for the phone.

"I was afraid you would be sleeping," Sonia said. "I am sorry to awaken you."

"That's all right. I had to get up to answer the phone anyway."

She pursed her lips in concentration—then smiled. "Ohh, a joke. Very good." The smile vanished. "It is important I call because you must return to London at once. This is a necessity."

"I'm not really finished here."

"I am sorry. But you will have to leave the work. It is hard to explain."

Jan had the sudden cold feeling that this was not her doing, that she had been ordered to recall him. He did not want to press her. "All right then. I'll get through to shuttle control and call you back . . ."

"That will not be needed. The flight leaves in about two hours and you have been booked on it. There will be time?"

"Yes, just about. I'll phone you as soon as I get in."

Jan broke the connection and turned on the lights, yawning and rubbing his prickly face. Somebody wanted him out of the station and back to London in a hurry. It had to be Security. But why? The answer seemed obvious enough. Men just don't disappear in space. Yet one had. Could it be that? He had the rather unhappy sensation that it was.

The return flight was an easy one—he was well adjusted to the sensation of free fall by now and he felt strangely heavy when he walked down the ramp on Earth. In a few days he had become used to the reduced gravity of the station. The Atlantic flight was equally uneventful, he slept most of the way. His eyes were gritty but he felt rested when he climbed from the plane in Heathrow. Outside was the world of weather again, and he hurried, shivering, to his waiting car where the attendant had left it. The thaw had finally set in and the snow was turning to slush. It still felt cold to someone acclimatized to a controlled environment. His coat was in the boot and he quickly pulled it on.

When he entered his apartment the first thing he noticed was the MESSAGE WAITING light on the phone. He thumbed the button and read the display on the screen:

I WILL BE WAITING IN MY OFFICE. SEE ME AS SOON
AS YOU ARRIVE.

THURGOOD—SMYTHE

171

It was no less than he expected. But Security, and his brother-in-law, could wait until he had washed and changed and put some decent food inside him. Rations at the station had been frozen, nourishing and boring.

While he was eating, Jan had the sudden thought that there was something else he could do when he saw Smitty. Right in the middle of Security! Dangerous, but hard to resist. When he emptied his pockets and changed clothes he managed to pick up a small device that he had constructed with some labor. Now he would find out how well it worked.

Security Central was a great, gray complex of windowless concrete buildings stretched along the north side of Marylebone. Jan had been there before and the central computer carefully remembered this fact. When he slipped his ID into the slot before the garage door, it returned it instantly to his hand and rolled open the door. He left the car in the visitors' bay and entered the lift which took him, under its own control, to the reception floor.

"Good afternoon, Engineer Kulozik," the girl behind the massive desk said, glancing at her screen. "If you will kindly take lift three."

He nodded and stepped through the security arch. There was a quiet buzzing and the guard looked up from the controls.

"Would you please step over here, your honor," he said.

This had never happened before. Jan felt a sudden coldness that he had to hide from the guard.

"What's wrong with the machine?" he asked. "I'm not carrying a gun."

"Sorry, sir. Something metallic in that pocket there. If you please."

Why had he brought it? What criminal bit of stupidity had led him to this folly? Jan put his hand slowly into his pocket and took out the device he had made and held it out before him.

"Is this what you mean?" he said.

The guard looked at the glow lighter and nodded. "Yes, sir. That's it. Lighters don't usually trip the alarm."

He bent to look carefully at it, reached for it. Jan stopped breathing. Then the man dropped his hand.

"Must be the gold plating. Sorry to bother you, sir."

Jan put his hand and the lighter into his pocket and nodded—he couldn't risk saying a word—and walked on to the open doors of the lift. They closed behind him and he relaxed, letting the lighter drop from his clenched fist. Close, entirely too close. He could not risk detection now by actuating the circuitry he had built into it. Far too dangerous.

Thurgood-Smythe sat behind the desk, unsmiling, and only nodded coldly when Jan entered. Uninvited, Jan dropped into an armchair and crossed his legs as casually as he could. "What's all this about?" he asked.

"I have a feeling you are getting into very deep trouble."

"I have the feeling that I don't know what the hell you are talking about."

Thurgood-Smythe leveled a finger like a gun, grimly angry.

"Don't try to play games with me, Jan. There's been another one of those coincidences. Soon after you arrived at Station Twelve a crewman vanished from one of the spacers."

"So? Do you think I had anything to do with it?"

"Normally I would not know or care. But the man was one of ours."

"Security? I can see why you're concerned."

"Can you? It is not that man but *you* I am concerned about." He counted slowly on his fingers. "You

173

have access to a terminal involved in illegal tapping. Then you happen to be in Scotland during trouble at a camp. And now you are present at the time a man disappears. I don't like it."

"Coincidence. You said so yourself."

"No. I don't believe in coincidence. You are involved in security violations . . ."

"Listen, Smitty—you can't accuse me like that, without any evidence . . ."

"I don't need evidence." Thurgood-Smythe's voice had the coldness of death in it. "If you weren't my wife's brother I would have you arrested on the spot. Taken out of here and sent to interrogation and—if you lived—to a camp. For life. As far as the world would know you would simply disappear. Your name would vanish from the public files, your bank account would cease to exist, your apartment would be empty."

"You could—do this?"

"I have done it," was the flat and overwhelming answer.

"I can't believe it—it's horrible. On your word alone—where is justice . . ."

"Jan. You are stupid. There is only as much justice in the world as those who are in control of the world care to permit, to enable affairs to run smoothly. Inside this building there is no justice. None at all. Do you understand what I am saying?"

"I understand, but I can't believe it could be true. You are saying that life as I know it is not real . . ."

"It isn't. And I don't expect you to take my word for it. Words are just words. Therefore I have arranged a graphic demonstration for you. Something you cannot argue with."

Thurgood-Smythe pressed a button on his desk as he talked and the door opened. A uniformed policeman led in a man in gray prison garb, stopped him by the desk, then exited. The man just stood there, staring unseeing into space, the skin of his face limp and hanging, his eyes empty.

"Condemned to death for drug offences," Thurgood-Smythe said. "A creature like this is useless to society."

"He's a man, not a creature."

"He's a creature now. Cortical erasure before execution. He has no consciousness, no memory, no personality. Just flesh. Now we remove the flesh."

Jan gripped the chair arms, unable to speak, as his brother-in-law removed a metal case from his desk drawer. It had an insulated handle and two metal prods on the front. He walked over and stood in front of the prisoner, pressed the prods to the man's forehead, and thumbed the trigger in the handle.

The man's limbs jerked once in painful sudden convulsion, then he dropped to the floor.

"Thirty thousand volts," Thurgood-Smythe said, turning to face Jan. His voice was toneless, empty of expression as he walked across the room and held the electrical device before Jan. "It might just as well have been you. It could be you—right now. Do you still not understand what I am saying?"

Jan looked with horrified fascination at the metal prods just before his face, their ends blackened and pitted. They moved closer and he recoiled involuntarily. At that moment, for the very first time, he was suddenly very frightened for himself. And for this world that he lived in. Up until now he had only been involved in a complicated game. Others could get hurt, he never would. Now the realization struck him that the rules he had always played by didn't exist. He was no longer playing. Now it was all for real. The games were over.

"Yes," he said, and his voice was hoarse. "Yes, Mr. Thurgood-Smythe, I understand what you are saying."

175

He spoke very quietly, barely above a whisper. "This is not an argument or a discussion." He glanced down at the body sprawled on the floor. "There is something you want to tell me, isn't there? Something that you want me to do—that I am going to do."

"You are correct."

Thurgood-Smythe returned to his desk and put the instrument away. The door opened and the same policeman entered and dragged out the corpse. Horribly, by the legs, bumping the limp head across the floor. Jan turned his eyes away from it, back to his brother-in-law as he spoke.

"For Elizabeth's sake, and for that reason alone, I am not going to ask you how deeply you are involved with the resistance—although I know you are. You ignored my advice, now you will obey my instructions. You will leave here and cease any contact, stop any activity. Forever. If you fall under suspicion again, are involved in any way with illegal activity—from that moment onward I will do nothing to protect you. You will be arrested on the spot, brought here, interrogated, then imprisoned for life. Is that clear?"

"Clear."

"Louder. I did not hear you."

"*Clear*. Yes, clear, I understand."

As Jan said the words he found a terrible anger driving out the fear. In this moment of absolute humiliation he realized how loathsome the people in power were, how impossible it would be to live with them in peace after this discovery. He did not want to die—but he knew he would never be able to live in a world where the Thurgood-Smythes were in charge. His shoulders slumped, and he lowered his face. Not in surrender, but only so that his brother-in-law would not see the rage, the anger that he felt.

His hands were thrust deep into his jacket pockets.

He depressed the button on the glow lighter.

The command signal radiated from the small but powerful transmitter inside. This activated the device concealed in the pen, clearly visible in the Security man's pocket. Upon receipt of this signal the memory bank was emptied and transmitted to the memory in the lighter. It took only microseconds. Jan let go of the button and stood up.

"Is there anything else—or can I go now?"

"It is for your own good, Jan. I gain nothing by this."

"Smitty, please. Be anything—but don't be a hypocrite." Jan couldn't prevent it; some of the anger leaked through. Thurgood-Smythe must have been expecting it because he only nodded expressionlessly. Jan had a sudden realization.

"And you hate my guts, don't you?" he said. "And you always have."

"That is absolutely true."

"Well—very good. The feeling is absolutely mutual."

Jan left then, not daring to say another word, afraid that he would go too far. He had no trouble leaving the building. Only when he was driving up the ramp did he realize what this meant.

He had gotten away with it. He had a recording in his pocket of all his brother-in-law's top Security conversations of the past weeks.

It was like carrying a bomb that could destroy him. What should he do with it? Wipe it clean, then throw the lighter into the Thames and forget forever what he had done. Automatically he turned the car toward the river. If he did anything other than this, it would be the utmost folly, a self-imposed death sentence.

The thoughts chased themselves through his head one after another and he could not think clearly. He almost ran through a red light that he did not see, would have run it if the car's computer had not caught his dereliction of duty and applied the brakes.

This was the sticking point, he realized. This was the moment when he determined what the rest of his life would be like.

He pulled the car into Savoy Street and braked to a stop, too occupied to drive. Nor could he sit still. He climbed out and locked the car, and started for the river. Then stopped. No, he hadn't made his mind up yet, that was the worst part. He still didn't know what he should do. He unlocked the trunk and rummaged in his tool box there until he found a pair of small earphones; he stuffed them into his pocket and turned toward the river.

A raw wind had sprung up and the slush was turning into rutted ice again. Other than a few distant, hurrying figures, he had the Victoria Embankment to himself. He stood at the stone rail, staring unseeingly at the ice floes in the gray water hurrying toward the sea. The lighter was in his hand. All he had to do was pull it out and throw it from him and the indecision would be over. He took it out and looked at it. So small, as tiny as a man's life.

With his other hand he plugged the earphones into the opening in its base.

He could still throw the thing away. But he had to hear what Thurgood-Smythe said in the security of his office, when talking to others of his kind. He had to know at least that much.

The tiny voices sounded in the privacy of his ear. Incomprehensible for the most part, conversations about matters, names he didn't know, complicated affairs discussed in a cold and businesslike way. The experts could have a field day with this, would be able to unravel and make sense of all the references and commands. It made hardly any sense at all to Jan. He jumped to the ending and caught some of their own conversation, then jumped back earlier in the day. Nothing of any real interest. Then he froze as the words sounded clearly:

"Yes, that's right, the Israeli girl. We've had enough trouble from her and we are going to finish it tonight. Wait until the meeting in the canal boat is under way and then . . ."

Sara—in danger!

Jan made the decision—unaware at the moment that he had even decided. He hurried, not running, that would be noticed, back to his car through the growing dusk. This evening—tonight! Could he get there first?

He drove coldly and carefully, making the best time possible. The canal boat. It must be the one on the Regent's Canal where they had met last time. How much did Security know? How did they know it? How long had they been watching their every move, toying with them? It didn't matter. He had to save Sara. Save her even if he did not save himself. She came first. The car lights came on as the sky darkened.

He must plan. Think before he acted. This car was probably sound bugged, so he had to treat it as if it were bugged. If he drove directly to Little Venice the alarm would be given at once. He would have to go part of the way on foot. There was a shopping complex on Maida Vale that would do. He drove in and parked and went into the largest shop. Through it and out the door on the far side, walking fast.

It was dark when he reached the canal. The lights were on along the towpath and a couple were walking toward him. He drew back into the shadowed protection of the trees and let them go by. Only when they

179

had turned out of sight did he hurry to the canal boat. It was tied in the same place, dark and silent. A man stepped out of the shadows when he climbed aboard.

"I wouldn't go in there if I were you."

"Fryer, I have to, it's an emergency."

"No way, old son, a very private meeting going on . . ."

Jan struck Fryer's hand from his shoulder, pushed him away so that he stumbled and fell. Then Jan had the door open and was jumping down into the cabin.

Sara looked up, eyes wide with surprise as he burst in.

So did Sonia Amariglio, the head of the satellite laboratories who was sitting across the table from her.

Twenty

Before Jan could react he was seized from behind so tightly that the air was driven from his lungs as he was dragged down.

"Bring him in, Fryer," Sara said, and he was released, pushed forward. "Close the door, quickly."

"You should not be here," Sonia said. "It is a dangerous mistake . . ."

"Listen, there is no time," Jan broke in. "Thurgood-Smythe knows about you, Sara, and he knows about this meeting. The police are on the way now. You have to get out of here, quickly."

They were stunned. Fryer broke the silence.

"Transportation won't be here for an hour more. But I can take care of this one." He pointed at Sonia. "The ice in the canal is still sound. I know a way out that way. But just for me."

"Get going then," Jan ordered. He looked at Sara. "Come with me. If we can reach my car we can start moving, stay ahead of them."

The light was out and the door open. As Sonia went by she reached out to touch Jan's face lightly. "Now I can tell you how wonderful the work has been that you have done for us all. Thank you, Jan." Then she was gone and they climbed the steps after her.

181

The towpath was still clear and Jan and Sara hurried down it.

"I don't see anyone," she said.

"I only hope that you're right."

They ran as fast as they could on the slippery surface, to the bridge over the canal. As they were about to turn onto it a car tore around the corner of the road, motor racing, and accelerated toward them.

"Under the trees!" Jan said, pulling Sara after him. "They may not have seen us."

Running, crashing through unseen branches, while the car grew louder and louder behind them. It hit the humpback bridge with a loud clashing of springs, was up and over, the headlights sweeping toward them. Jan fell face forward, dragging Sara down beside him.

The lights flashed past them and were gone. There was a metallic crash as the car turned into the towpath, riding down the sign that barred the way.

"Come on," Jan said, pulling Sara to her feet. "They'll start searching as soon as they find the boat is empty."

They ran down the first turning, running for their lives. At the next street there were pedestrians so they had to slow to a fast walk. There were more people about now—no sign of pursuit. They slowed to catch their breath.

"Can you tell me what you found out?" Sara asked.

"I'm probably bugged and whatever we say is being recorded."

"Your clothing will be destroyed. But I must know, now, what has happened."

"I bugged my dear brother-in-law, that's what. The biter bit. I have a recording, right here in my pocket, of all of his recent conversations. I couldn't understand most of it—but the last bit was clear enough. Recorded today. Planning to break up the meeting tonight on the canal boat. Those were his words. And he referred to 'the Israeli girl.'"

Sara gasped; her fingers dug into his arm. "How much can they know?"

"An awful lot."

"Then I must get away from London, out of this country at once. And your recording must reach our people. They must be warned."

"Can you do that?"

"I think so. What about you?"

"Unless they know I have been here tonight I'm safe enough." There was no point in telling her about the deadly warning he had received. Her survival came first. When that had been arranged he would worry about himself. "I've checked my car for optic bugs and it should be clean. Tell me now where you are going and don't talk again after we get in."

"The security barrier for vehicles is at Liverpool Road. Find a quiet street this side of it and let me out. I'm going into Islington."

"All right." They walked in silence for a moment, coming out of the side streets into Maida Vale. "The woman in the boat," Jan said. "What about her?"

"Can you forget you saw Sonia tonight?"

"It will be hard. Is she important?"

"Right at the top level in the London organization. One of the best people we have."

"I'm sure of that. Here we are. No talking now."

Jan unlocked the car and got in. He turned the engine and radio on, then muttered to himself. Getting out again he went and opened the boot and rattled his tool box, waving Sara into the car ahead of him. When she was seated he got in and drove slowly away.

Going down Marylebone would have been the most direct way, but Jan had no desire at all to go past Security Central. He turned instead toward St. John's Wood, through the quiet residential streets, then past Regent's Park. As he did so the music died away and a man's voice spoke loudly from the radio.

"Jan Kulozik, you are under arrest. Do not attempt to leave this vehicle. Wait for the police to arrive."

As the words crashed out of the speaker the engine died and the car coasted to a stop.

Jan's fear was mirrored in Sara's horrified eyes. Security knew where he was, had been tracking him, were coming for him. And they would find her as well.

Jan tore at the door handle but it would not move. Locked. They were trapped.

"It's not that easy, you bastards!" Jan shouted, rooting in the glove compartment for a roadmap, jamming in the cigar lighter at the same time. He pulled the map free and tore off a large square just as the lighter popped out. Holding the glowing element to the edge of the paper, blowing on it. It caught fire and he let it blaze, touching it to the rest of the map.

In a moment it was burning fiercely and he jammed it up behind the facia, in among the instruments and circuits.

The instant he did this the fire alarm began sounding and all of the doors unlocked.

"Run!" he said, and they jumped free of the car.

Once again they fled, not knowing how much time they had before the police arrived, running for their lives. Into the dark side streets, racing to put distance between themselves and the car. Running until Sara could run no more, then going on, walking as fast as she was able. There were no signs of any pursuers. Walking until they were in the safety of the crowded streets of Camden Town.

"I'm coming with you," Jan said. "They know all about me, about my connection with the resistance. I've been warned. Can you get me out?"

"I'm sorry I ever got you involved in this, Jan."

"I'm glad you did."

"Two people will be no harder than one. We are trying for Ireland. But you realize, if you do this thing, you'll be a man without a country. You won't ever be able to come home again."

"I'm that already. If they catch me I'm a dead man. Perhaps this way I can be with you. I'd like that. Because I love you."

"Jan, please . . ."

"What's wrong? I didn't realize it myself until I blurted it out just now. Sorry I can't be more romantic. That's my engineer's love song, I guess. And how about you?"

"We can't discuss this now, it's not the time . . ."

Jan took Sara by the shoulders, stopping her, moving them against a shop window. He looked at her, and lightly held her chin when she tried to turn away.

"There's no better time," he said. "I've just declared my undying love for you. And what do you respond?"

Sara smiled. Ever so slightly, but still she smiled, and kissed his fingers.

"You know that I am very, very fond of you. And that is all I am going to tell you now. We must go on."

As they walked he realized that he would have to settle for that. For the time being. He wondered what perverse streak had forced him to discover his love now, in this place, and declare it out loud like that. Well it was true, even if he had just admitted it to himself. True—and he was glad of it.

They were tired long before they reached their

destination, yet they dared not stop. Jan had his arm around her waist, supporting her as well as he could.

"Not much . . . farther," she said.

Oakley Road was a street of once elegant rowhouses, now derelict and boarded up. Sara led the way down the crumbling steps to the basement entrance of one of them and unlocked the door, closing and sealing it carefully behind them. The hallway was pitch black, but uncluttered, and they felt their way along the wall to the furnace room in the rear. Only when this door was closed did Sara turn on the lights. There were lockers along the walls, the welcome warmth of an electric fire, and the disused furnace in the rear. She found blankets and handed him one.

"All of your clothes, shoes, everything, into the furnace. They must be burned at once. Then I'll find you some clothes."

"You better take this first," Jan said, handing her the lighter. "Get it to your electronics people, Thurgood-Smythe is in the memory inside."

"This is very important. Thank you, Jan."

They had little time for rest. There was a knock on the door a few minutes later and she went into the hall to talk with the newcomer. After that they had to hurry.

"We have to get to Hammersmith before the buses stop running. Old clothes for both of us. I have some ID, won't stand up to anything more than casual interest, but we must have something. Is everything burned?"

"Yes, all gone." Jan stirred the red ashes with the poker, turning up the smoldering mass of his wallet. ID, papers, identification, his identity. Himself. The unthinkable had happened. The life he knew was over, the world he knew gone. The future an indecipherable mystery.

"We must go now," Sara said.

"Of course. I'm coming." He buttoned the ragged but heavy coat, fighting down the feeling of despair. He took her hand as they felt their way down the dark hallway, and did not release it again until they were out in the street.

Twenty-one

It was the first time in his life that Jan had been aboard a London omnibus. He had driven past them often enough without giving them a thought. Tall, double-decked, and silent, driven by the energy captured in the large flywheel beneath the floor. During the night thick cables would hook the bus to the electrical mains, using the powerful motor to run up the revolutions of the flywheel. During the day the motor became a flywheel-driven generator to power the electric drive motors. Reliable power, nonpolluting, cheap, practical. He knew that, the theory, but he hadn't known how cold the unheated vehicle could be, how littered with rubbish, thick with the smell of unwashed bodies. He held his bit of ticket and looked out at the cars that passed and vanished down the road ahead. The bus stopped for a traffic light and two Security police got on.

Jan stared straight ahead, just as the other people on the bus did, staring at the rigid face of Sara sitting across from him. One of the men stayed by the rear entrance while the other stamped the length of the bus, looking at everyone there. No one glanced his way or appeared aware of him.

The next time the bus stopped the two of them

left. Jan felt relief for a few moments, then the fear returned. Would it ever go away again?

They got down at the last stop, Hammersmith Terminal. Sara went ahead and he followed well behind as he had been instructed. The few other passengers dispersed and they were alone. Above them a car thrummed by on the elevated highway of the M4. Sara headed for the darkness of the arches that supported it. A small man with bent shoulders stepped out to meet her. She waved Jan to join them.

"Hello, hello, you nice people come with me. Old Jemmy will show you the way." The man's scrawny neck seemed too thin to support the globe of his head. His eyes were round and staring, his fixed smile empty of any teeth. He was a fool—or a very good actor. Sara took Jan's arm as they followed Old Jemmy into the totally dark and empty streets, among the rows of ruined houses.

"Where are we going?" Jan asked.

"For a little walk," Sara said. "Just a few miles they say. We have to get past the London Security barrier before we can get transportation."

"Those friendly police who used to salute me when I drove by?"

"The very same ones."

"What happened to all the houses here? They're in ruins?"

"London used to be much bigger, centuries ago, many more people. I don't know the exact figures. But population, over the entire country, was cut back to a smaller replacement level. Partly by disease and starvation, partly government policy."

"Don't tell me how they did it. Not tonight."

They were too tired to talk much after that. Plodding slowly after Old Jemmy who found his way unerringly in the darkness. He went even slower when lights appeared ahead.

"No talking now," he whispered. "Microphones about. Stay in the shadows right behind me. No noise neither or we're dead'uns."

Between two of the ruined buildings they had a brief glimpse of a cleared area ahead, well lit, with a tall wire fence down the center of it. They were very close when their guide led them into one of the buildings, an old warehouse of some kind. Out of sight of the road he produced a small flashlight and turned it on; they stumbled after the gleaming circle of light, deep into the ruins, down into the arched cellars below. He pulled some rubble and rusted sheet metal aside to uncover a door.

"In we goes," he said. "I'm coming last to close up."

It was a tunnel, damp and smelling of raw earth. Jan could not stand up fully and had to walk in a tiring hunched manner. It was long and straight and undoubtedly went under the Security barrier. There was muddy ice underfoot and they skidded across sizeable frozen puddles. Old Jemmy caught them up and passed them, leading the way again with his light. Jan's bent back was burning like fire before they reached the far end.

"Gotta keep quiet for a bit, like the other end," their guide warned as they emerged again into the frigid night. "A bit more walking and we're there."

The bit more was over an hour and Sara did not think she could make it. But Old Jemmy was far stronger than he looked, so he and Jan walked on each side of her, half supporting her. They were paralleling the motorway now and could clearly see the headlights sweeping by in both directions. An island of light appeared ahead in the darkness and they headed for it.

"Heston services," Old Jemmy said. "End of the line. You got a bit of shelter in this house here and you can spy from the window."

He was gone before they could even thank him. Sara sat with her back to the wall, her head on her knees, while Jan found the window. The service area was no more than a hundred meters away, bright as day under the glaring yellow lights. A few passenger cars were refueling, but most of the vehicles were heavy long distance lorries.

"We are looking for a juggernaut from London Brick," Sara said. "Is it there yet?"

"Not that I can see."

"We can expect it any time now. It will stop at the last hydrogen pump. When it does we get out of here. Past the buildings to the exit ramp, beyond the lights. The driver will stop there and open the door. That's our chance."

"I'll look out for it. You take it easy."

"That's all I can do."

The cold was beginning to bite through their heavy clothing when the long, articulated shape pulled in under the lights.

"It's here," Jan said.

There was more than enough light reflected from the area to show them a path through the rubble. They worked their way around it, then climbed the low fence. After that there was a cold wait behind a dark shack until the truck rumbled to a stop; the door swung open.

"Run," Sara said, stumbling toward it.

As soon as they were in, the door slammed and the great vehicle rumbled to life. It was wonderfully warm in the cab. The driver was a big man, half seen in the darkness.

"Tea in a thermos here," he said. "Sandwiches too. Get some sleep, if you want. No stops until we reach Swansea around five. I'll drop you before the Security check. Do you know the way from there?"

"Yes," Sara said. "And thanks."

"My pleasure."

Jan did not think he would be able to sleep, but the warmth and steady vibration of the cab lulled him. The next thing he was aware of was the hissing of air brakes as the driver drew to a stop. It was still dark out, though the stars were bright and clear here. Sara was sleeping curled against him, and he stroked her hair, reluctant to awaken her.

"This is the place," the driver said.

She was awake on the instant, opening the door when they stopped.

"Good luck," the driver said. Then the door slammed and they were alone, shivering in the cold hour before dawn.

"The walk will warm us up," Sara said, leading the way.

"Where are we?" Jan asked.

"Just outside of Swansea. We head for the port. If the arrangements have been made we will go out on one of the fishing boats. Transfer to an Irish boat at sea. We've used the route before successfully."

"And then?"

"Ireland."

"Of course. I mean the future. What happens to me?"

She was silent as they plodded on, their footsteps loud in the dark silence. "There has been so much to do to get out in a hurry, I just never thought. It might be arranged for you to stay on in Ireland under another name, though you would have to be very inconspicuous. There are a lot of British spies there."

"What about Israel? You will be there, won't you?"

"Of course. Your technical skills would be respected."

Jan smiled into the night. "Enough of this respect. What about love? You, I mean. I asked you earlier."

"This is still not the time for a discussion. When we are out of here, then . . ."

"When we are safe, you mean. Will we ever be? Are you forbidden to fall in love in your work? Or can you at least pretend to be to get some cooperation . . ."

"Jan, please. You're hurting me, and yourself as well, when you talk like that. I have never lied to you. I did not have to make love to you to enlist you in the work. I did it for the same reason that you did. I wanted to. Now, for a little while, let us please not talk like this. The most dangerous part is ahead."

It was a clear, cold dawn when they walked through the city. Other early risers were up, hurrying along, breath steaming. There were no police in sight. Security here was not as tight as in London. They turned a corner and there, at the end of the ice-slick street, was the harbor. The stern of a fishing trawler could be seen.

"Where do we go?" Jan asked.

"That doorway, it's the office. They'll know in there."

As they approached it the door opened and a man stepped out and turned to face them.

It was Thurgood-Smythe.

For a single shocking instant they stood, frozen, staring at each other. Thurgood-Smythe's mouth was twisted in a slight and unhumorous smile.

"End of the line," he said.

Sara pushed Jan hard; he slipped on the ice and fell to his knees. At the same time she drew a pistol from her pocket and fired twice, rapidly, at Thurgood-Smythe. He spun about and dropped. Jan was still climbing to his feet when she turned and ran back up the street.

There were Security Police there now, blocking her way, raising their guns.

Sara fired as she ran, over and over.

They returned the fire and she crumpled and dropped.

Jan ran to her, ignoring the guns pointed at him, lifting her and holding her in his arms. There was a smear of dirt and blood on her cheek and he brushed it away. Her eyes were closed and she was not breathing.

"I'll never know," Jan whispered. "Never know."

He held her still body to him, held her tightly, unaware of his tears. Unaware of the ring of police. Not even noticing Thurgood-Smythe who stood there as well, blood dripping between his fingers that he had clamped hard about his arm.

Twenty-two

The room was white, walls, ceiling, and floor. Unblemished and cheerless. The chair was white too, as was the plain table set before it. Sterile and cold, resembling a hospital in a way, but not like a hospital at all. Not at all.

Jan sat on the chair with his arms resting on the table. His clothing was white; white sandals were on his feet. His skin was very pale, as though it were trying to conform to the all-pervading whiteness. The reddened rings around his eyes were in stark contrast to the whiteness all about him.

Someone had given him a mug of coffee and it rested on the table, still held by his fingers. He had drunk none of it and it had grown cold. His red-rimmed eyes stared unseeing into the distance. There was no distance for the room was windowless. The door opened and a white-garbed attendant came in. He held a blast hypodermic in one hand and Jan did not protest, or even notice, when his arm was lifted and the injection was blown through his skin and into his bloodstream.

The attendant went out, but he left the door open. He was back in a moment with an identical white chair which he placed on the opposite side of the table. This time he closed the door when he left.

A few minutes passed before Jan stirred and looked about, then glanced down at his hand as though aware for the first time that he was holding the cup. He raised it and sipped, then grimaced at the cold liquid. As he was pushing the cup away from him, Thurgood-Smythe entered and sat down in the chair opposite.

"Can you understand me?" he asked.

Jan frowned a second, then nodded.

"Good. You have had a shot that should pick you up a little bit. I'm afraid that you have been out of things for some time."

Jan started to talk, but burst into a fit of coughing instead. His brother-in-law waited patiently. Jan tried again. His voice was hoarse and unsteady.

"What day is it? Can you tell me what day it is?"

"That is not important," Thurgood-Smythe said, dismissing the thought with a wave of his hand. "What day it is, where you are, none of this is of any relevancy. We have other things to discuss."

"I'll not tell you anything. Nothing at all."

Thurgood-Smythe laughed uproariously at this, slapping his knee with gusto.

"That's very funny," he said. "You have been here days, weeks, months, the amount of time is unimportant as I have said. What is important is that you have told us everything that you knew. Do you understand? Every single thing that we wanted to know. This is a very sophisticated operation that we run here and we have had decades of experience. You must have heard rumors of our torture chambers—but those are rumors we start ourselves. The reality is simple efficiency. With drugs, training, electronic techniques, we simply enlisted you on our side. You were eager to tell us everything. And you did."

Anger stirred Jan, stirring him from the lassitude that still gripped him.

"I don't believe you, Smitty. You're a liar. This is part of the softening up process."

"Is it? You must believe me when I tell you that it is all over. You have nothing more to say that I want to hear. You have already told us about Sara and your meeting on the Israeli submarine, your little adventure in the Highlands, at the space station. I said *everything* and I sincerely meant it. The people we wanted to apprehend, including Sonia Amariglio, a repulsive person named Fryer, others, have all been picked up and dealt with. A few more are still at large, thinking that they enjoy freedom. Just as you thought you did. I was very happy when you were recruited, and not only for personal reasons. We have plenty of small fry to watch, but they are not important. You led us into more rarefied circles that we wanted to penetrate. And we did. Our policy is simple: we allow these little groups to form these plots to be made and carried out, we even allow a few to escape. Sometimes. So our catch will be larger later on. We always know what is happening. We never lose."

"You're sick, Smitty. I just realized that. Sick and rotten and all the others like you. And you lie too much. I don't believe you."

"It is unimportant if you believe or not. Just listen. Your pathetic rebellion will never succeed. The Israeli authorities keep us informed of their young rebels who want to change the world . . ."

"I don't believe you!"

"Please. We follow each plot, help it to flourish, encourage the dissatisfied to join. Then crush it. Here, on the satellites, on the planets as well. They keep trying but they can never succeed. They are too foolish to even notice that they are not self-sufficient. The satellites will die if we cut off supplies. The planets as well. It is more than economics that has one planet mining, another manufacturing, another growing food.

Each needs the other to survive. And we control the relationship. Are you beginning to understand at last?"

Jan drew his hands down his face, felt them trembling. When he looked at the back of his hand he saw the skin was pale, that he had lost a good deal of weight. And he believed, finally believed, that Thurgood-Smythe was at last telling him the truth.

"All right, Smitty, you've won," he said with utmost resignation. "You've taken away my memories, loyalties, my world, the woman I loved. And she didn't even have to die to keep her secret. She had already been betrayed by her own people. So you've taken it all away—except for my life. Take that too. Have done."

"No," Thurgood-Smythe said. "I won't. I lied about that as well."

"Don't try to tell me you are keeping me alive for my sister's sake?"

"No. It never mattered for an instant what she thought, had no effect on my decisions. It just helped if you believed that it did. Now I will tell you the truth. You will be kept alive because you have useful skills. We do not waste rare talents in the Scottish camps. You are going to leave Earth and you are going to a distant planet where you will work until one day, in the future, you will die. You must understand, you are just a replaceable bit of machinery to us. You have served your function here. You will be pulled out and plugged in again some other place . . ."

"I can refuse," Jan said angrily.

"I think not. You are not that important a bit of machinery. If you don't work you will be destroyed. Take my advice. Do your work with resignation. Live out a happy and productive life." Thurgood-Smythe rose. Jan looked up at him.

"Can I see Liz, anyone . . . ?"

"You are officially dead. An accident. She cried a great deal at your funeral, as did a great number of your friends. Closed coffin of course. Good-bye, Jan, we won't be meeting again."

He started toward the door and Jan shouted after him.

"You're a bastard, a bastard!" Thurgood-Smythe turned about and looked down his nose at him.

"This petty insult. Is this the best you can do? No other final words?"

"I have them, Mr. Thurgood-Smythe," Jan said in a low voice. "Should I bother telling them to you? Should I let you know how indecent the life is that you lead? You think that it will last forever. It will not. You'll be brought down. I hope I'll see it. And I will keep working for it. So you'd better have me killed because I am not going to change what I feel for you and your kind. And before you go—I want to thank you. For showing me what kind of world this really is, and allowing me to stand against it. You can go now."

Jan turned about, faced away, the prisoner dismissing his jailer.

It penetrated, as nothing else had done that he had said. A flush slowly grew on Thurgood-Smythe's skin and he started to speak. He did not. He spat in anger, slammed the door, and was gone.

In the end, Jan was the one who smiled.

ABOUT THE AUTHOR

HARRY HARRISON, one of the most prolific and successful science fiction writers, worked as a commercial artist, art director and editor, before settling on a career as a free-lance writer. A past president of the World Science Fiction Writers' Association, Mr. Harrison was born in Connecticut and has lived in various European countries over the years. A recipient of numerous awards and honors, his *Stainless Steel Rat* books are as well known as they are humorous. His other books include *Deathworld, Deathworld 2* and *Make Room, Make Room*, his anti-utopian novel on which the movie *Soylent Green* was based. Harry Harrison now lives in Ireland.

FANTASY AND SCIENCE FICTION FAVORITES

Bantam brings you the recognized classics as well as the current favorites in fantasy and science fiction. Here you will find the beloved Conan books along with recent titles by the most respected authors in the genre.